Fortune Told in Blood

DAVUD GHAFFARZADEGAN

Translated and Introduced by
M. R. GHANOONPARVAR

The Center for Middle Eastern Studies
The University of Texas at Austin

Cover photograph: Christopher Rose
Cover design: Kathy Phan & Kristi Shuey
Series Editor: Wendy E. Moore

Library of Congress Control Number: 2008923609

ISBN: 978-0-292-71839-5

The Center gratefully acknowledges financial support
for the publication of *Fortune Told in Blood* from the
Society of Iranian American Women for Education.

Table of Contents

❖

Acknowledgments

❀

I am grateful to Faridoun Farrokh for his thorough reading of the translation and for his indispensable editorial help. I would also like to express my gratitude to Wendy Moore and Nasrin Rahimieh for their valuable suggestions. As always, I am most indebted to my wife, Diane, who has been a guiding light throughout the completion of this project.

Introduction

In 1996, when *Fal-e Khun* [Fortune Told in Blood] was originally published in Persian, the eight-year Iran-Iraq War, the longest war in the twentieth century, had been over for almost seven years; Saddam Hussein of Iraq, who started the war, was still in power; and both countries were trying to cope with the loss of human life and the destruction caused by the war. The Iran-Iraq War began in the wake of the Islamic Revolution in Iran, and following a long history of border disputes between the two countries. When Iraqi forces invaded Iran on September 22, 1980, they did so without a formal declaration of war or any warning; but after the initial shock, Iran was able to consolidate its military forces, which were in a state of relative disarray as a result of the revolution and change of regime, and prevent the enemy from making major advancements. For almost eight years, both sides claimed supremacy in various battles and each side predicted its imminent victory in the war, but as the weeks, months, and years went by, neither side could see any gains, and losses amounted to over a million casualties and tremendous destruction. By August 20, 1988, when the two countries agreed to a ceasefire, Iraq had been criticized for its use of chemical weapons against Iranian military troops and civilians, as well as Iraqi Kurds, and Iran for its use of "boy soldiers," among other things.

The diplomatic conflict over the Iraq-Iran border, which occasionally led to military action, has a history several centuries long. In the mid-sixteenth century, when the Ottoman Empire conquered the territory that comprises modern Iraq, as its neighbor to the east, Iran was considered the empire's rival. After World War I when Iraq was made a separate state, serious disagreement developed between Iran and Iraq regarding the border between them, in particular concerning the river known as the Shatt al-Arab by Arabs and the Arvandrud by Iranians, which divides the southern parts of the two countries and is Iraq's only access to the open ocean, through the Persian Gulf. Despite various agreements regarding the border in 1937 and 1975, relations between the two nations remained problematic for numerous reasons, including the fact that although Iraq is predominantly Arab and Iran is predominantly Persian, on both sides of the border there were divided political loyalties: the Kurdish population in the north, the Arab minority in the Iranian province of Khuzestan, and the largely Shi'ite population of Iraq, which shares the same faith with the majority of Iranians.

When the Islamic Revolution of 1978–79, under the leadership of the Shi'ite cleric Ayatollah Khomeini, overthrew Mohammad Reza Shah and the Pahlavi dynasty, relations between the two countries continued to deteriorate. The Iraqi government, under the control of Saddam Hussein, feared the political rhetoric espoused by the newly established Islamic Republic of Iran, which seemed to advocate a similar religious revolution and government for Iraq. And the weakened state of the Iranian army, the result of purges, along with the international crises that Iran faced, including the severance of relations with the United States due to the hostages taken from the American embassy, further tempted Saddam Hussein and his government to invade, thus beginning a prolonged war between the two neighbors.

The war inevitably forced both countries to draft conscripts to supply their troops, which suffered high numbers of casualties. While the Iranian side relied mainly on its larger population and revolutionary zeal, Iraq was in a more dire situation in regard to recruits due to its smaller population, despite receiving military and diplomatic help from other states such as Egypt, Saudi Arabia, and Jordan, among others. Iraqis, though perhaps motivated by certain nationalistic sentiments, were increasingly skeptical about the promised outcome.

As the war went on, soldiers on both sides gradually and increasingly became aware of the senselessness of the conflict. Regarding the Iranian side, this sense of futility is reflected in the works of many filmmakers and fiction writers. *Fortune Told in Blood* is an attempt by Davud Ghaffarzadegan to project the same sense of futility onto the Iraqi side.

As in all wars, each side began the conflict convinced that it was right and that God was on its side. Each side believed itself to be fighting for Islam and Muslims and regarded its adversary as inhumane infidels. As a result, much of what was produced in Iran in the form of poems, stories, and of course films during the war directly or indirectly served as war propaganda, dealing with themes such as self-sacrifice and martyrdom, and while depicting Iranians as embodiments of these virtues, they presented a dehumanized picture of the enemy. During the war, a significant number of war films with such themes were shown nightly on television.

But there were also antiwar films, such as *Bashu, Gharibeh-ye Kuchek* [Bashu, the Little Stranger], by the renowned film director Bahram Beyza'i (though its distribution was not allowed until the early 1990s). Another film which dealt with the effects of the war on the soldiers who fought it was Mohsen Makhmalbaf's *Arusi-ye Khuban* [The Marriage of the Blessed] (1988).

Antiwar fiction was also produced during the war. Examples include Qazi Rabihavi's *Vaqti Dud-e Jang dar Asman Dideh Shod* [When the Smoke of War Was Seen in the Sky] (1981), Nasim Khaksar's *Man Solhra Dust Daram* [I Love Peace] (1981), Qodsi Qazinur's *Vietnam Gavahi Ast* [Vietnam Is Proof] (1980), Ahmad Mahmud's *Zamin-e Sukhteh* [Burned Land] (1981), and Esma'il Fasih's *Zemestan-e 62* [Winter of 83] (1987), which expressed the sense of frustration, helplessness, and desperation felt by Iranians suffering the death and destruction caused by the far-reaching effects of modern warfare on their cities and villages. *Fortune Told in Blood*, however, goes one step further. It humanizes the Iraqi enemy. This aspect of Ghaffarzadegan's work can be regarded as a positive development, especially in the context of the animosity that was ignited by the anti-Iranian rhetoric of Saddam Hussein and his regime, which started the war and named it "the second Qadesiyyeh" (a reference to the seventh-century Battle of Qadesiyyeh when the Islamic Arab army invaded the Persian Empire). In the spring of 1995, when Davud Ghaffarzadegan completed the writing of *Fortune Told in Blood*, perhaps enough time had passed for the extremely hostile emotions to subside to some degree and for both nations, or at least many people in both countries, to begin to view certain human attributes in their adversary, in a sense to humanize the enemy.

Fortune Told in Blood is an internal novel for the most part, but it is also a story of the interaction between two individuals from different classes: an ordinary conscript from a lower-working-class Iraqi family and an educated officer, also a draftee. But they also have much in common. They look to the future with both hope and uncertainty, and in the course of their close association on the top of a mountain where they have been assigned as lookouts for enemy troop movement, they begin to know each other, as well as themselves. They learn about loyalty to their country and government, but also, more importantly, about loyalty to each other as human beings. They have been cast into an extraordinary situation in which their courage is tested, but they also face, and are tested in terms of, what they come to realize is the meaning of life, with regard to their own individual but also collective human existence. *Fortune Told in Blood* is a story of death and destruction, but as the characters confront death, we also find a confrontation with life and an understanding of its value.

In many ways, it is also a story about dreams and aspirations, albeit unfulfilled.

The humanization of the enemy can of course be seen in Ghaffarzadegan's choice of characters and the story he tells. But it is also addressed by the character of the young soldier who, from a distance and through binoculars, can empathize and even identify with people he is supposed to regard as enemies.

Davud Ghaffarzadegan was born in 1959. In other words, during the Iran-Iraq War he was young enough to have been conscripted or to have volunteered, neither of which occurred. He was born in the city of Ardabil, in East Azerbaijan province. His first language is Azeri Turkish, but he writes in Persian. He is a teacher by profession, and has published over twenty-five novels and collections of short stories, many of which have received literary and artistic prizes. Among his short story collections are *Ma Seh Nafar Hastim* [We Are Three Persons], *Raz-e Qatl-e Aqa-ye Mir* [The Secret of the Murder of Mr. Mir], and *Dokhtaran-e Delriz* [The Delriz Girls], and his novels include *Sayehha va Shab-e Deraz* [Shadows and Long Night]. Ghaffarzadegan is also known as a writer of books for children and young adults, including two collections of short stories, *Hezarpa* [Centipede] and *Mu Ferferi* [Curly Haired], and three novels, *Parvaz-e Dornaha* [The Flight of the Cranes], *Sangandazan-e Qar-e Kabud* [The Blue Cave Stone Throwers], and *Avaz-e Nimeh Shab* [Midnight Song].

Ghaffarzadegan has a special facility with the Persian language. Very economical with words, he can vividly depict a scene with a few strokes of the pen and the inner workings of a character's psyche with a short phrase. Although he has described himself, as have critics, as a writer who is interested in the art of storytelling rather than trying to convey a particular message, in recent years he has gained the respect of critics and readers as a significant literary figure concerned with social issues, and while his reputation as an established writer began with his writing for children and young adults, he also says that when he writes he does not think about a particular age group as his readers. What he is interested in is the art of fiction.

In terms of genre, *Fortune Told in Blood* can best be classified as a novella. Although it seems that in the English-speaking world, perhaps because of its seemingly awkward length, the novella as a subgenre has not been as popular as the short story and the novel, some of the most important literary artists in modern Persian literature have chosen this form for their work. For instance, Sadeq Hedayat's *Buf-e Kur* (published in the late 1930s and translated into English as *The Blind Owl*), which is perhaps the most widely translated, read, and discussed work of Iranian fiction, is a novella. Similarly, other important writers such as Mohammad Ali Jamalzadeh, Bozorg Alavi, Jalal Al-e Ahmad, Hushang Golshiri, and more recently Shahrnush Parsipur and Mohammad Reza Bayrami, to mention a few, have utilized this form. Golshiri's most popular masterpiece, *Shazdeh Ehtejab* [Prince Ehtejab], and Parsipur's *Zanan bedun-e Mardan* [Women without Men] are both novellas that also appear in English translation.

The reasons for the popularity of the novella in Iran perhaps include the type of readers that authors envision. Reading is still not a habit and a hobby for the majority of Iranians, despite the increasing literacy rate in recent decades. It appears that while many Western writers write for the general public, Iranian writers for all intents and purposes cannot yet hope for such a wide audience. Moreover, nonliterary factors such as the shortage and high price of paper since the Islamic Revolution have also contributed to the inclination of Iranian publishers and writers to favor this subgenre.

Ghaffarzadegan's novella was published in a climate in Iran where many veterans of the war were gradually beginning to look back and reassess the conflict and their own role and place in society. With the experiences of thousands of young people, many of whom were trying to cope with their disabilities, their time as prisoners of war, and other consequences of the war, a new discourse began among the veterans that divided them into two camps, which has continued to the present. One camp consists of those who still adhere to the political and ideological rhetoric of wartime, i.e., referring to the conflict as the "sacred defense" and the "imposed war," and consider it a sacrilege to question the reasons for it. The other group is comprised of those who are trying to look back at the war and their experiences with a more sober outlook. To the first group, the members of the second are regarded as traitors to the idea that the Iran-Iraq War was the "war between good and evil," the Islamic Republic and Saddam's regime. One critic from the first camp, for example, even reprimanded the translator of Ahmad Dehqan's *Journey to Heading 270 Degrees* for translating what he considered a heretical novel, which appeared in the same year as *Fortune Told in Blood*. This was the social climate in which Davud Ghaffarzadegan's novella was published. Given that Ghaffarzadegan is not a veteran of the Iran-Iraq War, to some extent his book was disregarded by the first group of critics, while praised by readers in the second camp, and it went through a second printing in less than a year.

To better familiarize the reader with the writer of *Fortune Told in Blood* and the scope of his work, a translation of a journal interview appears at the conclusion of this volume.

The translation is based on Davud Ghaffarzadegan's *Fal-e Khun*, 2nd printing, Mo'asseseh-ye Entesharat-e Qadyani, 1376 [1997]. The transliteration of Persian names and terms is based on Persian pronunciation.

Fortune Told in Blood

Chapter One

❊

He was looking back, his legs trembling, thinking that death here would be awful: dizziness, dry mouth, and the cold sweat that runs down your spine.

How could the Lieutenant jump around on the rocks so happy and vibrant? Every few steps that he took, he would stop and jokingly shout, "Come on, come on . . . !" with a shrill, happy, childish voice and pink lips out of which puffed his breath in the cold.

The Lieutenant's voice made him nervous. He did not know why. Perhaps because he himself was afraid of heights and could see that the Lieutenant was not afraid at all. Perhaps after all this time he had become accustomed to seeing the skull under the skin on the heads of everyone and seeing that all this vitality, enthusiasm, and life would not last more than a few days, and that it would turn into cold, rotting flesh collecting all sorts of bugs and maggots.

All he could think about was death—it had become a habit for him—and if he were not so self-conscious in the presence of the Lieutenant, he would drop to the ground all the junk that they had loaded on him and stuff his fingers into his ears not to have to hear the overpowering echo of the laughter of death from the bottom of the valley.

The higher he went, the more difficult it was to negotiate the climb. He slipped on the snow, took a fleeting look behind him, and trembled to the core in fear. Now he was farther away from the Lieutenant, who was standing in the middle of the snow, his arms akimbo, looking around.

He took several quick steps and pulled himself up a slippery frozen rock. He should not look back. The Lieutenant bent over, picked up a fistful of snow, and threw it at him. The snowball hit him right on his shoulder strap. He laughed in response to the Lieutenant's playfulness. He did not know what his reaction should be. He had never been on close terms with a superior or engaged in the horseplay common among soldiers.

It was the first time that he had met the Lieutenant and had gone on an assignment with him. He might have seen him before many times, but nothing special had happened to make him remember his face.

These were his instructions: Accompany the Lieutenant up the mountain for observation duty.

Prepared, as usual, he had gotten himself together promptly, gone to the Lieutenant, and clicked his heels. The driver had floored the gas pedal. When they reached the side road, the Lieutenant lit a cigarette. In the closed, smoky atmosphere inside the jeep and from behind the muddy plastic window, the plain, dark and gray, was disappearing behind them. How far they had traveled, he could not remember. Before them and behind them mortar rounds had plowed the ground. The jeep bounced up and down in the ditches and sped forward. He held firmly to the cold bar under the canvas roof to keep from being tossed around. The area was new to him, and he had never been so close to a mountain.

He thought: If someone gets shot and falls down to the ground in this snow and ice, what will his face look like? Will the corpse swell up like in the marshlands or not? And the rats . . .

Perhaps he was thinking about these things now, but in the jeep he had thought about other things. He realized that he had no memory of the road and did not remember what the driver looked like. Did he have a round face, or was his face long, like the Lieutenant's? He only remembered a lock of hair on his forehead, and a neck that was so black and thick that it looked like a log. Or perhaps he had seen that curly lock of hair and the thick neck somewhere else, and now that he was standing on the slippery rock and shivering like a dog, he was making up these things. But whatever it was or whomever it belonged to wasn't important. The Lieutenant had delicate facial features and a thin neck, and he was wondering why a person so thin and scrawny should now be in the middle of the fighting . . . He remembered now; it was the driver's neck that was so thick and had a bluish tint. When the driver had turned around toward him with a cigarette between his lips, he had seen his yellow teeth and his roving, lustful eyes. He had abandoned them in the middle of the hills, and without a word had rapidly turned the steering wheel and left them, like the wind.

The Lieutenant, standing with his hands on his hips, had watched the jeep leave as he made a whistling sound. Then he had looked around and gazed at him with a childish smile.

The air down below was clean and mild, without the heaviness and harshness of the air up in the mountains. There was neither a chill, nor a wind sweeping the snow from the base of the rocks and blowing it on your face. Everywhere was calm, sparkling clean and silent. In the place where they were standing among the hills, nature was pristine, like the first days of Creation, or so he had thought: At the beginning of Creation, everywhere must have been quiet, silent, and clean. With a thick vapor moving in the air and . . . But he realized that that was not the case. All his imaginings were bits of ideas that he had borrowed from one person or another, and he had never himself had the time to be alone, in solitude. Some sort of permanent, gnawing anxiety existed in him; had he worked like a dog and struggled so much just to come up a mountain with this guy and have his knees get so weak that he could hardly move?

Down below, he had had the opportunity for a few minutes to look around and observe everything carefully. He had put the equipment down on the ground and waited to see what the Lieutenant had to say. The Lieutenant was looking at the plants and trees and the small stream passing nearby. He seemed to be preoccupied with the sound of it. Standing with his hands on his hips, he listened intently, his eyes wandering slowly here and there.

He stood motionless, watching the Lieutenant out of the corner of his eye, but the Lieutenant did not seem to be thinking about getting on the way very soon. He walked a few steps away from the Lieutenant and went and stood by the stream. He looked around and did not see anything interesting, except the awesome presence of the mountain. He thought: You have to be crazy to get excited at seeing a few blades of grass in this situation.

He jumped to the other side of the stream and went among the bushes. He came back and saw the Lieutenant still standing, his hands at his hips, in a daze. He shrugged his shoulders. When he started to walk, the dry leaves crunched under his feet. He squatted next to a bush. He was amazed to see the diversity of color in the leaves. It was as if he had come from another planet and this was the first time he had seen a leaf or seen that grass is green and rocks have color and mass. It seemed as though in these two or three years since he had put on the soldier's uniform he had not thought of anything but death. He said to himself: If death is like the falling of a leaf from a tree, then that is also some sort of experience. In a way, it is coming from the earth and going back to the earth. Then why be so afraid of it?

No, it was not the fear of death. It was the fear of the pathetic kind of dying. Becoming cannon fodder. He could not quite find the words for it. Dropping dead like an animal, perhaps. Yes, that was it. The humiliation of a death that is imposed on you.

He could not help it. These were the things that he thought about all the time. From the first day that they had brought him to the region . . . In the marshlands he was mostly afraid of the rats that devoured the corpses. And the nightmares: He saw that in the middle of a cane field, water was slowly moving his swollen corpse, and large gray rats with sharp teeth and small pink paws were sitting on his chest, wet and stinking, chewing his flesh. First they would chew his nose, his ear lobes, and his cheeks, and then his lips and the base of his throat, and from there, they would dig a hole to the inside, which was rotting.

Every time he passed through a cane field on a boat, he saw corpses in that condition. And from night until dawn, he was soaked in a cold sweat inside the sleeping bag that he would zip up past his neck. He would not dare bring his head out. Frequently, he had felt the rapid movements of the rats on the canvas cloth of the sleeping bag, and muffled his screams.

When he stood up next to the dry leaves, he said to himself: What would rats be doing here in this snow and cold?

He felt light, and joyfully ran in the leaves. He stood on the top of a large rock, and beneath the awesome presence of the mountains he thought about his dreams. Why were his nightmares so often about falling into bottomless chasms? Were his dreams not meant to warn him? Then why one moment—only for one moment—when he was getting out of the jeep had he felt that he had seen this place before? Whatever it was, it was familiar. That was what terrified him so much. These hills, this mountain peak covered with snow, and this Lieutenant with his foolish behavior seemed strangely familiar to him.

He thought the end could come anywhere. That fateful moment. And now that he had been freed from the nightmare of man-eating rats, perhaps something far more difficult and more ferocious was awaiting him.

When the sound of the jeep had faded away, he had felt as though he had been abandoned somewhere remote and isolated, like a leper. He hadn't known what to do. The presence of the Lieutenant was nothing to be counted on. Whether he was there or not was all the same. Here there was neither the sound of shots and rifles nor shouting and orders. Nothing of the miseries of war had spread to this pristine place—they were supposed to open a new front. There was silence, just silence. Only that narrow murmur flowing by the trees under a thin layer of melting ice, from which wisps of steam arose. And the song of an unfamiliar bird chirping in the distance.

Behind the hills, illusive and mysterious, was silence in the midst of a thin fog, and on this side—where he and the Lieutenant were standing—it was so clear that it seemed like an enchanting, incredible dream. Perhaps he had had this dream many times, standing among a few hills, the air shimmering like a mirror because it was so bright and clear. There was neither tormenting heat nor biting cold. A few clumps of white cloud floating on the horizon and a bird flying toward the sun, a song flowing from its small beak. And he, in harmony with nature, standing under a generous shower of light. Like a man with no past or future. Floating in the present. Immersed in the sunlight. When had he had this dream?

In the marshlands, he was inundated with death and destruction. The air was stifling, the maddening heat stagnant. Everything seemed futile and in vain. The boat split the water, slithering calmly through the cane field. The guys were sitting on both sides of the boat quietly, in a state of readiness. The waterway was narrow and full of twists and turns. At any moment, they could be caught in an ambush, their chests suddenly showered with bullets.

He was sitting at the bottom of the boat with his finger on the trigger, watchful of everything around him. An insatiable thirst tormented him. When they turned around the bend of the first waterway, they saw the swollen black bodies of their comrades, partially devoured by rats and fish. Thin, waving lines of veins floated on the water, and the undersides of the bodies that had been eaten away were nauseatingly white. A boat with a hole had capsized near the corpses, half sunk in the water and stuck in the mud.

They drove further, and cautiously approached the corpses. They had to retrieve them as soon as possible from the water and go back.

This was the first time that he had touched a soaking wet, slimy corpse. Up to that moment, he had been stifled by the heat, but suddenly a deep chill shook his bones, and an odor filled his nose that he had never smelled before, a smell that darkened the mind and filled the mouth with bitter bile. When they moved the first corpse, several large rats swam away into the bamboo. From then on he had the nightmare of the rats, rats that devoured human flesh, getting fatter every day. Fat, healthy rats, soaking wet gray rats with constantly moving narrow snouts . . .

The sound of the Lieutenant's whistling brought him back. How long had he been standing there? He picked up his weapon and jumped off the rock onto the snow. Why should he think about corpses halfway up this mountain? The Lieutenant was looking at him, smiling. He stomped on the snow and ran. The Lieutenant laughed louder and extended his arms toward him, as if encouraging a toddler to take a step or two.

He felt his ears burning with embarrassment. But he saw that the Lieutenant was not close enough to see his red face. He gestured to the Lieutenant to go on, and crept forward quietly. He bent over, shifting his weight forward. He was so afraid of falling. His fear was excessive and unnatural, because the Lieutenant, who seemed to have been brought up pampered, was pulling himself up the mountain easily and nimbly, and when he stopped to take a breath, he would again start to whistle.

The sound of an artillery gun far away resonated loudly, but was muffled by the mountain. They had only reached the halfway point. The closer they got to the peak, the deeper the snow, and there were fewer places to secure their hands and feet as they climbed. Leaning on the rifle, he pulled himself up slowly and cautiously. His body was hot, and the blood seemed as if it would gush out of his veins. He wished they would reach the bunker as soon as possible and rest. He felt that up there would be safe and inaccessible. His only misgiving involved the Lieutenant. He did not yet know what kind of man he was. Up to this point, he had found him to be simple and harmless. He could not believe that an officer could be so easygoing and mellow. He thought that the pleasantness of nature had overwhelmed the Lieutenant, and that when on duty, he would be no different from others of the same rank. But what was the difference? He had gotten used to getting along with any sort of person. And there was no other way. He only wanted to reach the bunker more quickly. He had read somewhere that they had found a Vietnamese or some other soldier in the jungles who was still hiding years after the war. He had stayed in the jungle and lived there. They had his picture in the newspapers. A thin man with narrow eyes, staring at the camera in amazement. Why should they drag such a human being out of his nest? Was it only fear? No, it was not just fear. There must have been other things, too . . .

There are other things, too. How can you say it? If only there was someone to write for him. He had no one. But that lock of hair on the forehead. Where had he seen it?

No, he did not want to die. That lock of hair surely belonged to someone with an enticing, desirable, and reproachful look. Where was she waiting for him? He should not let the rats disfigure his face. How would he know that they were not here as well? They were everywhere. Under the fire of artillery guns and mortars. The appetite for human flesh had driven fear from their hearts. They hung around everywhere, sniffing, with their narrow snouts and needle-sharp teeth. His body still felt tired from the road when he saw them. He had not had a chance to turn around to see where he was.

An order had arrived: Go to the front immediately!

He knew that they were not joking. He even knew this behind the lines. They were not joking with anyone. It was war. Death squads with light machine guns were hanging around everywhere—khaki-uniformed rats behind the bunkers—and the generals and the colonels with their fists full of commendations and medals and their pockets full of execution orders all said the same thing: Go and die!

Everyone's fate in dying was different. Everyone had their own kind of death. He had seen this many times. The soldier who always put his feet outside the bunker—he remembered how the shrapnel had hit him right in the chest. He did not even have a chance to say, "Ouch." Even if wounded and crippled, he wanted to stay alive. It rarely happened that shrapnel hit you right in your heart, when you were lying down. But the soldier had not known that death was waiting to ambush him. A death that was his alone. No one else's. Several others were also there, and they were not even lying down. And that little piece of hot lead was not their fate. It belonged to someone else. That delusional, unfortunate, negligent . . .

Like in his childhood when he thought that everyone had a star in the sky. And everyone's star only belonged to them. And when a star traveled in the sky and burned out—just like tracer bullets—someone's life would come to an end. He wanted to know what his fate was. When he looked at the corpses, he tried to guess how the fellow must have fallen. He imagined how he must have suffered the throes of death, and the trembling at the last moment, and the arms that get twisted. The lifelong dreams that suddenly come to an end.

There's not a thing you can do about it. It is a visitor that knocks at everyone's door.

If he were lucky, the bullet would hit his heart or forehead. Or a flying or burning piece of shrapnel would lop his head off in an instant. And he would run no more than a few steps. Before the still open, surprised eyes of the fallen head. And the gushes of blood from the throat. Only a few steps. The splattering of blood in a strange land. And the head would be silenced. The eyelids would drop. The face, if it was not mutilated, would begin to turn yellow, and the horror of death would petrify it, and the earth would fill the silenced mouth from between the half-open lips, and the body would fall to the ground a short distance from the severed head. The trembling of the legs and the grinding of the heels in the ground, once or twice. The pulsating of the still warm flesh of the muscles, the vibrating of fingers, and then silence . . .

These were good deaths; they were lovely; he had assessed all aspects of them.

Lovely death. That's right! But perhaps not desirable. A long, blissful life. The leisure time of old age. Offspring, children. How good it would be to leave the world satisfied. Like they show in the movies. By the way, why had he not written his will yet? He kept postponing it. Maybe when he got up there he would have the time; but no, he was afraid. He had no intention of dying. Why should he write his will? For whom? Perhaps for that lock of hair on the forehead. Better for her to be waiting—if it was not all a dream and imagining.

Movies and stories are nice. Especially stories: Once upon a time, there was a kind old man who had no possessions in this world except for a daughter as beautiful as the sun. The ruler of that country regarded everything good as belonging to him. As fate would have it, one day . . . He wished that he could remember the whole story. He knew that it had a happy ending. Like the endings of all stories, lovely and appealing.

The young get their wish and the old shut their eyes from the world with peace of mind. Why should one be raised with such trifles?

What if these things did not exist? For sure life would be an empty, horrifying abyss, and there would be nothing but affliction, nothing but disgrace and death. And herds of people constantly led to slaughter. Yes, stories are indeed nice. And this pristine nature spread before him now, does it resemble anything but a story? These mountains and this white, cold, bright snow lying on the ground, what else are they? If only war were not dragged to such places and they would allow this mountain, in its ancient mind, to continue to stand proudly and watchfully.

Only their footprints were evident in the snow. The track of his boots and the Lieutenant's, who was walking ahead of him. He thought that the Lieutenant's boot size was probably seven or eight. What delicate feet!

He started walking faster. His knees were less shaky now, and he could climb the ridge of the mountain more easily. As if the mountain had accepted him on its back. He was advancing on bits of rocks, and with every step he was getting closer to the Lieutenant. There was still no sign of the observation bunker. Surely they had concealed it well and the snow was helping to make it even less conspicuous. Better that way.

A thought crossed his mind: Since the mountain overlooks the area so well, why should the enemy forces not be here? Their scouts might also be here. They might be hiding behind a rock and waiting for an opportunity.

He stopped and took a look around. He squeezed his weapon in his fist. He did not see anything suspicious and did not hear a sound, except the quiet whispering of the wind shaking the dried bushes.

The Lieutenant had also stopped and was looking at him. His face had turned serious; he seemed to be worried. He went behind a rock and took a look around through his binoculars. He stood up and laughed, then turned his back to him and resumed climbing.

Why was he showing his fear so much? He felt disgusted with himself. He had never been able to conceal his fear from others. He was always like an open book. He was like that even when he was a child. His mother would quickly catch him doing something wrong and go after him with a broomstick. He would run around the courtyard and finally take refuge on the roof. His mother would not follow him up there. She would threaten him from where she was standing downstairs, and then she would go about her own business. Relieved, he would lie down on his back and gaze at the sky. He liked to see the birds fly. And he would make up stories for himself with the shapes of the clouds. It would already be nighttime when he would come back from his daydreaming, and then it was the turn of the stars appearing in the sky: That big one belongs to Mother. This one that is twinkling is Father's star. It was twinkling to say that Father had gone on a trip.

A journey of no return. He was eleven when he figured this out. His mother had deceived him all those years. A journey just like the trip that he was on now. But what mother would tell her child where his father had gone? He had not thought about this at all.

How did the others swallow their fear? Their true faces would only be revealed at the moment of death. The same people who up to a few minutes ago were chatting were now struggling. Terrified, they were looking for a shelter to save their lives. They would ask the rocks to give them shelter. Out of fear, they were digging the ground as if they were digging for a treasure. They were asking the soil for protection to no avail, and like prey caught in the claws of a predator, they were being torn to pieces in a strange land. Their heartrending cries split the dome of heaven, and there was no one to come to their rescue. The area would be calm again, they would bury the ones that had been killed, and those whose lives had been spared would again start chatting and joking, without a care.

He had heard that those who are most afraid of death are only those who have a strong imagination, because the horror of death seems so enormous to them.

Chapter Two

The Lieutenant was so oblivious to the situation that he did not notice his arrival. He was standing with his hands on his hips, looking ahead. His hat was squished in his hand, and he had thrown his backpack in the corner of the bunker. A look of disbelief was on his smooth face, frosty breath emitting from his nostrils.

He tossed the radio transmitter and the equipment next to the Lieutenant's backpack. He bent down and took a look inside the bunker. It seemed like a warm, cozy place to him. He stood up again and saw the Lieutenant looking as stunned as before. As though he had no idea that he could be in range of the sharpshooters.

He coughed to let the Lieutenant know that he was there. He was still panting, and sweat was running down his spine. Involuntarily, he took off his hat and gazed at the scenery before him. As if he were standing in front of a painting. He thought he was dreaming. But no, it was not a dream. Whatever it was, it was real, and with open eyes he was witness to the most beautiful view of his life.

He moved forward a little and stood at the edge of the precipice. On this side, the mountain was like a straight wall; it seemed impossible for anyone to climb. He felt secure. The precipice faced the enemy forces, so there would be no danger from them. He held on to a rock and looked down. He felt dizzy. He closed his eyes for a moment and then opened them again. The canyon was deep and rocky, with sparse underbrush growing among the sharp rocks. No, no one could climb up from this direction. Unless he was a mountain goat or some sort of ghost. He looked ahead again. A stream encircled the mountain and was wider on this side. As far as the eye could see was an expanse of dark green grass studded with small and large trees, and farther on, it seemed that a black column was passing through the trees and advancing forward. A village could be seen behind the tall poplar trees. Silence pervaded the scene and there was no sign of military forces anywhere that could be seen with the naked eye. Except for that black column that continued to advance like ants and turned behind the hills. Perhaps they were villagers who were leaving their homes with all their possessions and animals.

He pulled back from the edge of the precipice. The sweat had dried on his body. Up here, the air was colder and more biting; it stung the skin on his face. He put on his hat and took another look at the Lieutenant, who was checking the surroundings through his binoculars. He rubbed his hands together and walked toward the bunker.

The air inside the bunker was stifling and stagnant and smelled like leftover food and sweat. Empty food cans were piled up in a corner, and the floor of the bunker was covered with cigarette butts and trash. He sat on the ammunition box and thought about what changes he could make inside the bunker to make it pleasant and comfortable for two people. He saw that, other than the trash that needed to be cleaned up, everything was in order and ready. The main thing was food and fuel, which they had enough of for a few days; for light, there was a sooty lantern hanging from a wooden post. So, as the first task, he gathered the cigarette butts and the trash and shoved them under the corner of a blanket. Second, he filled the lantern with kerosene and lit it. The soft yellow light of the lantern made the place cozier. It looked like they had come to a vacation home in a village with a pleasant climate. Only a third task remained. He lifted the blanket that covered the opening of the bunker. He would have to let in some fresh air. Now everything was ready; it was just right for leaning back and having a good time. He checked around inside the bunker. He found a deck of dirty, dog-eared playing cards and a few old soiled magazines. The cover of one of the magazines had a full-length picture of a slender-waisted, tall woman, with delicate calves and a short skirt, advertising stockings. Behind her was the blue sea, and she was looking sideways at an unknown spot. A lock of golden hair happened to have fallen on her smooth, tanned forehead.

He stacked the magazines and placed them on the box. He picked up the cards, shuffled them a few times, and stuffed them into the small pocket of his backpack. He spread two blankets on the floor of the bunker, and felt his stomach growling badly. It wouldn't be polite not to wait for the Lieutenant. He rolled the cans on the blanket. The small glassy eye of a fish head pictured on one of the cans stared at him. He kicked the can into a corner with the tip of his toe. What did the eye of the fish remind him of? He didn't feel like thinking. Now that after so long a time he had found a cozy, quiet corner, he wanted to relax without any concerns. He picked up a can of pineapple juice and opened it. He took a few sips and the bitter taste in his mouth went away. He always enjoyed drinking a cool beverage. But here, it seemed that he would prefer a cup of tea or coffee. He felt like having tea, hot, with a sharp aroma and a bitter aftertaste. He finished the pineapple juice reluctantly. Just the first few sips were tasty. He crushed the empty can in his fist and threw it outside the bunker. The can dropped noisily on the rocks and rolled down. What a noise it made, the damned thing. It sounded like an empty metal washbasin thrown from the roof onto the cobblestones of an alley on a warm, quiet afternoon. For several moments, he could hear the tin can rolling on the rocks. From one rock to the next. It was probably jumping into the air, too. How long would it take for it to reach the bottom of the canyon? He thought: A man is heavier and would get snagged more easily.

The Lieutenant rushed in fuming, holding back an insulting comment he wanted to make. He said that by now he should have realized what it meant to be on watch, that if he did not, from now on he would have to be very careful, or he would have to teach him . . .

He was taken aback by the swift and sudden action of the Lieutenant. He pouted and avoided his eyes. He said to himself: Did I not say that all of these mother . . . are cut from the same cloth?

Now the Lieutenant was standing with his hands on his hips, looking at the provisions inside the bunker. The binoculars in his right hand seemed suspended in the air, and his face had once again assumed a look of childish innocence.

"Great . . . !"

He felt overjoyed seeing all those magazines, the various colorful cans of food, and the full cans of kerosene. He turned around inside the bunker and pulled out a book, the corner of which stuck out from under the pile of blankets. He placed the binoculars on the box and curiously leafed through the pages of the book.

"Guess what I found . . . a sacred Chinese book!"

"What can we do with it?"

"We could tell our fortunes with it. It's good entertainment."

He placed the book on the magazines, picked up the map of the region, and left the bunker, binoculars in hand.

"It seems like something's going on around here."

He had never associated with such a person. What an animal! First, he had made him upset, and then, like nothing had happened, he had gotten so excited at seeing a used, torn book. He could go to hell!

Again he went back to the food cans. He felt thirsty and wanted some tea. The fruit juice had made him thirstier. He squatted by the Coleman cooler and drank several glasses of water, one after another. The water was old and warm, but it was satisfying. He wiped his lips with his sleeve and went out of the bunker. He looked around for a piece of clean snow that had not been stepped on to put in the Coleman. The whiteness of the snow was spotted with yellow holes and zigzagging lines. He thought: This is what soldiering is all about, a mess . . . Like gypsies, one day we are in this bunker, and the next day we have no idea where we'll be. Maybe in the ground. The yellowness of the urine is because of the fear of death more than anything else.

Depressed, he walked back to the precipice. The Lieutenant was sitting behind a rock, looking around through the binoculars and marking the map. He stopped behind him, squatted down, and held the edges of the map that were flapping in the wind. The Lieutenant smiled at him.

"I couldn't find any rocks lighter than three or four kilograms around here. And as you see, I'm not an athlete."

He looked around through the binoculars and marked the map again and again with red X's. When he finished his work, he got up. He rolled up the map and explained the status of the area. His index finger was fixed for a moment on the black column slowly passing behind the trees.

"I think they're nomadic tribes, perhaps our own."

He handed him the binoculars.

"Come, look!"

Then he started walking toward the bunker.

"Did you get the radio transmitter going?"

He watched the Lieutenant walk away, and he saw the sky, which was all white and overcast. He breathed a sigh of relief. He felt his heart was trembling with joy. He did not know why. Seeing clouds always gave him peace of mind. Like a wall that distanced him from the violent and unpleasant world of reality and shielded him, away from sorrows and joys.

He turned and looked at the dark opening of the bunker into which the Lieutenant had disappeared, and now he could only hear him whistling and working on the radio transmitter. As if he had no concerns. If he were like him, how easy his life would pass. Da dum, da dum . . . Can you just hum a tune and snap your fingers? I guess everyone is different. It depends on what you're made of. No concerns.

He looked around through the binoculars. He started from the bottom of the boulder he was standing on and moved forward slowly. Everywhere was slippery and frozen, with sharp black rocks. He crawled forward from rock to rock. He always liked strange, unknown places.

He wanted to make a mental record of the area, inch by inch. It was better than the Lieutenant's paper map that could be blown away by the wind or burned in fire. How colorful were the moss- and snow-covered rocks through the clean lenses of the binoculars. He took pleasure in looking at them bit by bit.

He raised the binoculars. Now it was a different view, an unknown land that seemed to be empty of inhabitants. How could one be sure that the enemy was not lurking behind the rocks? He did not see anyone as far as the edge of the stream, no creatures. But the wind was moving the branches, and higher up the birds were flying fast. He crossed the stream. If only he could step into the water. The pleasure of rolling on the soft, moist grass . . . The sound of water splashing under his boots . . . Through the binoculars, he had not gone more than a few steps when he came back. He always paused for a little while next to water. He loved to look at the pebbles on the bottom and see the water roll on its course. No, rolling is too harsh. Flowing. Flowing, soft, and sliding. His eyes stopped on a small, short tree next to the stream. How solitary! This is my tree, drinking from my stream, getting warmed by my sun, and getting nourishment from my rich soil. No one should hang around it. My tree! He felt a strange sensation in his heart. He thought: If this tree falls one day, I will also be one of the fallen. Our fates are bound together. If I fall, it will also . . . He regretted not having chosen a large tree with deeper roots. Since falling is what is in store, oh well. Death, again. He thought that it was all too late. Everyone only has one chance in life to choose. The tree had done its job; when in my life did I have the choice? Always . . .

If only he had wings. He would fly over the cliff and build a wall around his tree. He would place rocks around it so everyone would know that his tree was off-limits. But how far the tree was! On the other side of the border mountain, in the land of the foreigners. He thought: Then how could this be my tree? Surely it has an owner. Or maybe it's a free tree. It just felt like growing next to a stream. Maybe it was marked by one of the tribesmen or one of the villagers, and he would eventually return one day, look at it and say: How big my tree has become! A tree that he might have planted on the day that his child was born. And maybe that child will be with him, or maybe he will have fallen, or maybe he will have taken off and gone to some place far away.

He realized he had no tree at all. He was all alone. But as for a star, yes, he still had one. Because he was standing alive at the edge of the precipice and looking down through the binoculars. Then, he was still there and he still had his lucky star.

He gave up on the idea of "my tree." He had crossed the stream and was looking for any sign of the enemy between the thorn bushes and rocks. No, there was nothing. Everything seemed like an illusion. He went further. The enemy should be there. Otherwise, what were they doing with all those weapons and guns? He was walking slowly, cautiously. The leaves crushed under his feet. He ran to the last tree and hid behind it. Before him, there was a row of mud houses, vague and fuzzy, as if enshrouded in smoke and fog. He adjusted the binoculars. How empty the alleyways were! But no, it seemed that a horse with a long, disheveled mane was passing by. It was galloping so fast. He lowered the binoculars. His eyes had grown weary from roaming around so much. Maybe I have become delusional. He looked again. No, it was there. Chickens and roosters were clawing the ground. What a pity that he could not go to the alleyway behind. He thought: I wish I had wings. Two wings, like pigeons. He flew over the first roof. Suddenly he faced an old man with a long moustache who was aiming his muzzle-loading rifle at him.

It was not worth the risk. He quickly turned the binoculars. He passed over the village hastily and started shadowing the black column that was advancing slowly across the plain. He could hear the sound of the sheep bells. Men dressed in black, with their heads tucked into their collars, were creeping forward slowly. All in a line following each other. In one column, in a long line that had no end. Like a silhouette photograph of a camel caravan on a plain, but it was strange since it was not sunny here.

He sat on a rock. He placed the binoculars on his knees. What was this place he had come to? He was at a loss for a few minutes, in a daze. He was not dreaming or imagining. He got up and walked in the other direction. He looked at the friendly forces on the plain through the binoculars. Along the path that they had climbed with difficulty, he went down rapidly and stopped. Precisely where the Lieutenant had been standing with his hands on his hips, whistling. He crossed the stream, and again the crunching of the leaves. No, he did not want to think about death anymore. He saw the shadow of death in everything that he came across. And now it was the beginning and the end. He dropped his head. He was tired. But he had to be certain. He had to be sure that what he saw was not an illusion. He looked through the binoculars at the road along which he had come in the jeep. Full of twists and turns. And the plain was still dark and dreary. Farther away, the camp of the friendly forces, bunkers being dug, and artillery. His ears filled with the chirping of the tank wheel tracks. It was strange. It was as if the lenses of the binoculars also brought sounds closer. Like the rocks, the herds, and the soldiers.

He placed the binoculars on a rock. Like a scary object. He turned his head toward the bunker. It was not clear what the Lieutenant was doing in there. He was still whistling, and he could hear the sound of things being moved around. He started walking toward the bunker. He had left the binoculars behind. Frustrated, he went back and picked them up. Closer to the bunker, he heard the Lieutenant's voice. He perked up his ears. The Lieutenant was reporting the status of the area on the radio. Then he heard him giving the location and saying with a laugh: "For now, two . . ."

His knees weakened. He did not go inside the bunker. He went back and again stood at the edge of the precipice, and looked at that black line that had been drawn continuously on the plain. Again, his eyes fell on "my tree." Even though he was convinced that it could not be his tree, he liked to say "my tree" and think that he had something that he could call "mine." He shut his eyes. He heard the faint sound of an artillery gun. The air vibrated and the howling resonated in the silent plain, creating a horrifying echo in the hills. He opened his eyes. The sky was full of crows. They were flying in every direction toward the horizon. They were flapping their wings, frightened, and they were crowing. And the black line was still there, determined and undeterred. It continued moving forward, calmly and slowly.

When he heard the second shot, he closed his eyes. It was better to keep them shut. Where had he read that the prophet of some tribe always sat with his eyes shut under some tree?

He threw the binoculars on the snow drift and made fists with his hands in his pockets. If only he could go and sit under "my tree" with his eyes shut.

When he opened his eyes, he saw the Lieutenant standing

face-to-face with him and looking at him astonished.

He said: "Just testing!"

And he started walking, a shy smile on his face.

"These tribal people are capable of anything. These herdsmen."

The Lieutenant said "herdsmen" with contempt. But his voice was trembling.

"You aren't a village boy?"

He stood behind the Lieutenant.

"No!"

"I didn't want you to be offended."

"They won't bother us."

"Just testing. I wanted to be sure."

"It could have been different."

"Our war is with them."

"Our?"

The Lieutenant turned to him in surprise.

"Yes, yours and mine."

And then he went into the bunker.

Why had the Lieutenant disturbed the tranquility of the place? He lit a cigarette. He wanted to relax comfortably in the bunker.

A cold wind was blowing and icy droplets of water hit his face. He did not like to smoke facing the wind. It made it hard to breathe. He turned his back to the wind. He looked up and saw that the sky was closer than anything else. A thick fog was creeping forward from behind the mountains, heavy and compressed, filling the valley.

He threw the cigarette to the wind. Now the cloud was right above his head, and if he stretched his arm he could grab a chunk of it in his fist. The fog was coming forward. It was moving toward him, and it was about to reach the top of the bunker.

The wind died down a little and dancing flickers of snow suddenly began to fall. He had only seen snow falling a few times before. Joyfully, he ran around and called the Lieutenant.

The Lieutenant rushed out of the bunker with his gun in his hand, but when he saw the dancing snowflakes, he put the gun aside and ran toward him, put his hands on his shoulders, and they began a foot dance together in unison.

The snowflakes were getting bigger every moment.

The Lieutenant lifted his face to the sky and stuck out his tongue, panting. The snowflakes fell on his red tongue and melted. The Lieutenant's antics made him laugh, but when he tried it himself and felt the coolness of the snow on his warm tongue, he realized how pleasurable it was.

The snow was falling so fast that they could not even keep their eyes open. The flakes hit their eyeballs and hurt. He said to himself: If only it was always like this. Happiness.

His heart was filled with confidence and joy.

Now the wind was also mingled with the snow, and they could not stand up straight. They ran into the bunker. They closed the steel plate of the opening and drew the curtain. The first thing was to turn up the flame of the lantern and warm up the air inside the bunker. The snow on their heads and shoulders was melting, and the Lieutenant's face was so clean that it sparkled.

"If only we had a window."

"What?"

"A window. It's fun to look at the snow falling from behind a window."

The Lieutenant said this, picked up the fortune-telling book, and sat down. He moved close to the Lieutenant and stared at the book in his hands.

The Lieutenant said: "You can't do it on an empty stomach."

He then shut the book and looked at his face.

"Good thing you reminded me; my stomach is growling, too."

He picked up a few cans of food and sat down. Carefully, he opened the cans with a bayonet and emptied the contents into a frying pan and placed it on the kerosene heater: eggplant, caviar, and beans.

He sat by the heater and stirred the food with a spoon. The Lieutenant was once again checking out the Chinese fortune-telling book. He was holding the book with one hand and reading it, and with his other hand he untied his bootlaces. He took off his boots and tossed them by the opening of the bunker. He pushed the blankets under him, just like a hen in a chicken coop about to lay eggs.

"It's like I haven't eaten for years," the Lieutenant said.

He removed the frying pan from the heater and put it on the box in the middle of the bunker. He opened two cans of orange juice and tastefully placed them on two sides. He then arranged the forks and spoons next to the fruit juice cans.

"Sir!"

The Lieutenant shut the book and moved forward with a smile.

"We need more light."

He brought the lantern closer. Now half of the bunker was lit and the other half was dark. Everything was ready. The Lieutenant's eyes exuded kindness, and steam rose from the food and mingled with the aroma of spices.

They picked up their forks and spoons unhurriedly and began to eat. The Lieutenant took small amounts of food.

"You know," the Lieutenant began, "I'm a law student. The last year . . . if we hadn't had this war."

"But we do!"

"Yes, unfortunately."

The Lieutenant took a sip of his orange juice while he swallowed a greasy mouthful of food, which he had not chewed thoroughly.

"We have land. It's from my dad."

"Do you farm it?"

"No, I've leased it. I wanted to study literature."

The Lieutenant made no response.

He had not eaten in such comfort and with such peace of mind for a long time. Food in bunkers always sat heavily on his stomach, and every bite that he took he thought was his last. Smiling, he looked at the Lieutenant's hazel eyes while chewing a mouthful of food. He was trying to be well-mannered, like the Lieutenant.

The Lieutenant said: "You can't count on anything at all. A law student . . . But now I'm here . . . You know, I have a fiancée!"

He stopped chewing for a moment. The wind was howling outside and the biting cold was penetrating through the cracks of the opening of the bunker.

"She's only eighteen."

He dropped his head. At that moment, he did not want to look into the eyes of the Lieutenant. He drank his fruit juice halfway and picked up the empty pan of food and set it aside. The Lieutenant had stretched out his legs and was trying hard to light his cigarette with the flame of the lantern.

He put his hand in his pocket to get a cigarette. The Lieutenant was faster, though, and offered him one of his.

Face-to-face, leaning on the sandbags, they smoked their cigarettes without a word. The blue aromatic smoke of the cigarettes spiraled upward in the soft light of the lantern in the closed, half-lit atmosphere of the bunker.

The Lieutenant put out his cigarette and got up energetically.

"Well. We've got the book and magazines. And in my backpack, I have a cute little radio made in Japan with a little red light . . . This is the life! To hell with the university and law."

The Lieutenant's words made him feel good. He pulled his backpack toward him, took out the playing cards, and placed them on the box.

The Lieutenant whistled: "One gets greedy and wants other things, too."

He turned and turned the dial on the radio. Soft music

filled the bunker.

He leaned against the wall of the bunker, and turning to the Lieutenant, he said out of the blue: "It's like I'm dreaming. I'm always dreaming. Dreaming of the rats . . ."

The Lieutenant lit another cigarette. "With the snow that has started, God knows how many nights you'll have to dream."

The Lieutenant's words made him anxious. He got up and looked outside. The snowstorm blew into the bunker. He latched the door quickly and dropped the blanket that served as a curtain over it.

The Lieutenant said, laughing: "To hell with it. We've got everything: water, food, fuel . . ."

"I got worried for a moment."

The Lieutenant turned up the radio: "We have a radio transmitter; we'll let them know. Just pretend that we've come on vacation. Like two old friends. In the Swiss mountains. One can endure anything. It depends on one's personality."

He placed the radio on the ground and picked up the fortune-telling book.

There was silence for a few minutes. He was still standing. The snowflakes had melted on his face. He picked up the playing cards and shuffled them, inviting the Lieutenant to play.

The Lieutenant was busy with the book.

"We need three coins. All the same size."

And he added:

"I never carry change in my pocket. I don't like the sound."

He took out his change and dropped it on the box in front of the Lieutenant.

"So you also have Iranian money!"

"I took it as a memento. Along with this ring."

He held out his hand and showed the turquoise ring.

"The guys strip the corpses. I only liked this ring. This change had fallen on the ground. It belonged to a kid, twelve or thirteen years old."

The Lieutenant said nothing.

"The ring was too big for his finger. He had wrapped it with a piece of cloth."

The Lieutenant said: "Get a pen and a piece of paper!"

He put the playing cards on the table and took out a pen and a piece of paper from his backpack. He shouldn't have talked about the ring. The wounded face of the kid appeared before his eyes. He licked the stone on the ring and rubbed it against his chest.

The Lieutenant shouted: "You're not supposed to rub turquoise! It is not agate, you know."

He dropped his hand. He said: "They are strange people."

The Lieutenant raised his head and looked at the turquoise ring.

"They risk their lives before gunfire without a second thought."

The Lieutenant remarked sarcastically: "Because they're kids."

"Even if they're kids, they're strange kids. They're not like us when we were children."

"Under this sky, everything is alike."

"I still can't believe it. They were two kids. Thirteen or fourteen years old."

The Lieutenant raised his head: "Who?"

"They had headbands on their foreheads. We could see them quite clearly. We could plant a bullet right between their eyebrows."

The Lieutenant said: "What are you talking about?"

"You would not believe it. They had come all that way to take the calf."

"I have no idea what you're talking about."

He looked into the Lieutenant's eyes.

"We were behind the embankment. The cow had fallen in the open field and the wind carried its mooing. It mooed somehow like a person in pain. Shrapnel had taken off its leg."

"Well, things like that happen."

"No. We thought they had come to put it out of its misery. One of them was sitting down and caressing the neck of the cow. It was then that we realized that the cow was giving birth. My friend was a villager. I wanted to shoot them; he did not let me. He said, 'Jackass! Aren't you human?'"

The Lieutenant shifted his position and shut the book.

"Can you believe that?"

The Lieutenant said: "I told you, they're kids."

"No. My friend was cursing everything. They were only two kids, with dark complexions and red headbands. They had come to save the calf's life in the middle of all that mess."

The Lieutenant smiled softly.

"Don't ruin our day."

"When the calf was born, they wrapped it in their shawls and took off."

"You were lucky they didn't come after you."

"No, they only wanted to rescue the calf. The cow was done for."

"I told you, things like that happen."

"I didn't steal this ring. I only wanted to have it. That's all."

The Lieutenant's eyes glided past the ring to the coins.

"Well, let it go . . . This book predicts the future. But your question must be clear and specific. And this is not a gypsy game."

He hesitated. He did not know what to ask. He had never been in such a situation, so serious. Once a gypsy woman had read his palm and said, "The world is not kind to anyone, but you have good luck. You will marry three women, and when you get old your children will take care of you. And you will also make a lot of money."

The Lieutenant repeated what he had said. He was rolling the coins in his hand and looking at his mouth.

"Ask!"

"What should I ask? I don't know."

"I'm sure you have something to ask. Some trouble, a wish, or, for example, love . . ."

"The future?"

"Yes. Ask whatever you want. The answer is in here."

Yes, he had a question. Why should he not ask about death? How was he going to die? Here, and everywhere else, the future consisted only of death. Only the form of death would be different. Death by direct shot, by stepping on a mine, by drowning, or by falling . . . falling from a height, and many other forms of death. As many as the number of stars. No harm in asking. Maybe he had found someone with the answer.

He said: "I have my question."

"If it's not a secret, tell me. I want to see how the answers will work out."

"I want to know how I will die . . . even when."

The Lieutenant was taken aback: "Death?"

He was at a loss for a moment. The look on his face had changed. As if full of shadows.

"Strange!"

"What's strange? It's the only thing that one can be sure of. Only its form differs. Just as I said, death!"

"Couldn't you ask a good and proper question? About love and falling in love, for example?"

"I have no one. I don't remember anything. It's as if I have no past. I only want to know how I will die. The way I want it, or with difficulty . . . I'm afraid of the rats."

"Rats?"

"I don't want them to disfigure my face."

"What difference will it make? In the end, we'll all die one way or another."

"I want to know exactly 'how.'"

The Lieutenant gave up. The coins were in his hand.

"Why did you ask that they be hit by artillery fire?"

"Who?"

"The villagers, or, I don't know, the tribespeople. A bunch of old men and women."

"Wars are not all peaches and cream."

"But they were minding their own business. They weren't bothering us."

The Lieutenant waved his hand in frustration.

"Enough, already!"

"Like I said, I want to know how I will die."

The Lieutenant held out the coins to him: "Roll them in your hand and drop them on the box. Only think about your question. You must concentrate. You must throw the coins six times."

And then he pulled the pen and the piece of paper toward him.

He did not know why he wanted to tease the Lieutenant.

"You can't tell a fortune with these coins. Enemy coins are supposed to be bad luck."

"It looks like you're being stubborn. When we go back down, watch out. No one likes this type of joke."

He rolled the coins in his hand and tossed them on the box.

The Lieutenant looked and said: "Two heads and one tail."

He then drew a straight line on the paper.

He rolled the coins in his hand again and again, six times, and each time the Lieutenant took notes. Now he had made six horizontal lines.

The Lieutenant put aside the piece of paper and the pen and opened the book at a page with a chart.

"I found it. Listen: 'Fire on the mountain. Distance and separation. This is the fate of the traveler. Two men in search of shelter under the branches and leaves of a large tree. The fire of the camp of the migrants is visible in the distance. Tomorrow—it will not be there.'"

The Lieutenant raised his head.

"That's all."

"I didn't get any of it."

The Lieutenant laughed.

"I didn't understand anything either. But it was strange, wasn't it?"

"Maybe. How about yours? Don't you want to test it? It might give you the right answer. The way you want it, the way you hope it will be."

"I wanted you to die before me. I'm afraid of predictions. The future frightens me. I prefer to live in the moment."

But he picked up the coins and rolled them in his hand. He paused, and asked: "What did you mean earlier? After all, it's war. It doesn't matter who they are. It doesn't make any difference whether they are old or young. Why did you take a kid's ring? What would you call this action? Maybe he wanted to die with that ring."

A shiver ran down his spine. He had provided the Lieutenant with an excuse to pick on him for no reason.

"We are in a foreign land. There is a tree here that belongs to them," he said abruptly.

The Lieutenant closed his eyes.

"In war, nothing belongs to anyone. Only everyone gets a share in dying. And what is written in books is nonsense. Old wars were more fair and humane."

"Yes. In those times they would not shoot people from the top of a mountain."

The Lieutenant frowned. With a bitter smile, he said: "You're looking for your fortune for no reason. I can see what your fate will be with my eyes shut: field trial on the charge of treason to the homeland."

And he began to laugh madly. His eyes had filled with tears, and he could not stop himself from laughing.

He lowered his head to avoid looking at the Lieutenant's disgusting red face. Laughing, the Lieutenant rolled the coins in his hand and tossed them on the box. Before noting anything down, he said: "I also asked the same question as you did. The main question is: 'To be or not to be?'"

He continued: "Don't take it to heart. I just said it so you would watch yourself. These are bad times. You should know all this, because you're interested in literature."

And again he rolled the coins and tossed them on the table.

"Well, now let me see what it will tell me."

He had opened a page and was reading quietly.

"It's nonsense. See what it says: 'A container full of moving insects. Worry. Working on what is decayed. Great negligence and destruction.'"

He shut the book and threw it into a corner.

"It's nonsense. It's so cold here that you cannot find insects."

And he laughed nervously.

"It's all your fault. You got us upset."

"You said yourself that it's a credible book."

The Lieutenant stuck his hand in his pocket and took out a cigarette.

"Who has ever been able to predict the future? What has been fabricated and written in this book can be interpreted in a thousand ways."

He felt he wanted to be free of the Lieutenant for a moment. He was short of breath. He wanted some fresh air. He got up to leave.

The Lieutenant shouted: "Where are you going?"

With his back to the Lieutenant, he said: "I want to see whether or not the fire of the migrants' camp is visible from here."

Chapter Three

Half asleep, he heard the Lieutenant's voice. "Get up, someone is coming up."

Confused and sleepy, he opened his eyes.

"Get up!"

He sat up and looked at the pale face of the Lieutenant.

"Someone is coming up the mountain."

"Who?"

"I don't know. I can't tell."

The Lieutenant picked up the binoculars and left the bunker quickly.

He did not feel like getting up. Where he was sitting was warm and cozy, but outside was cold and icy. In the course of these two days, he had become accustomed to the idiosyncrasies of the Lieutenant, to his talking in his sleep, to the sudden silences, and to his . . . Once the Lieutenant laid his head on the blanket, he would start snoring, and after a few minutes he would begin arguing and quarreling. His face would perspire and then suddenly he would wake up and sit up. And no matter how much he thought about it, he could not remember what he had been dreaming about. No more than a few moments later, he would once again sprawl on the ground, and once again there was snoring and quarreling.

The Lieutenant slept like a sparrow. Early in the evening he would doze off, and early in the morning, with rosy cheeks, while brushing his teeth with fruit juice, he would begin to sing and whistle. He would no longer be the quarrelsome man that he was when he was sleeping. He would become cheerful and tame, aside from the sudden silences that seemed to drown him—he would crouch up silently for half an hour and would not talk.

He wriggled under the blankets. He thought: This must be another one of the games that the Lieutenant plays. He's jealous of my sleeping so much.

All this time, even though they were warm and comfortable in the bunker and they did not worry about the war, still it seemed that there was something wrong.

Their nest on the top of the mountain and under tons of snow was safe, and the days and nights passed without any concern for war and peace. Yesterday, when the snow stopped, the clouds moved away and the sky became entirely clear, blue and translucent. But the bitter, biting cold covered everything with a sheet of black ice.

The first night they went to bed early, perhaps because of the anxiety and apprehension caused by telling their fortunes. The snow was falling heavily and it was impossible to go outside the bunker. You could not even see one step ahead. They arranged to take watch every three hours. They drew lots for the first watch, and his name was drawn. The Lieutenant happily crawled under the blanket and started snoring. He picked up the radio, which was next to the Lieutenant's ear, and brought the lantern and placed them next to him. He was bored and he wanted to occupy himself somehow. He shuffled the playing cards and tried to tell his own fortune. He set aside the extra cards and arranged the face cards in front of him: The girl has lost her heart to the boy, but there is also someone else involved. That stinks . . . He tossed the cards into a corner. The Jack of Hearts landed on his knee. Which girl? And the other person? Where had he seen that curly lock of hair? That lock of black hair? He could not remember. Nothing at all. Neither a face nor a glance. Only a curly lock of hair . . . He picked up the Chinese fortune-telling book. He read the introduction but could not understand a thing. He could not concentrate. The chart and the notes confused him even more. He thought this was also some sort of diversion for upper-class people. Like the card playing of young people who have just come into some money, and gypsy palm readers for old maids and those whose luck has turned.

But what was in this book was strange. It did not make any promises. It had occasional consoling drawings and mysterious Chinese characters full of twists and turns. The drawings of cranes in long flight, a fat man wearing a kimono with his hands on his knees, next to a pond full of water lilies . . . A bewildered man in a cane field unwittingly stepping on the tail of a sleeping tiger. A lion sleeping in the woods with its snout displaying sorrow and ferociousness. A woman with heavily coiffed hair and wide sleeves kneeling on the ground with her hands under her chin . . . The more he turned the pages, the more confused he became. Can one predict the future with these sketches?

He was tired, but he could not fall asleep. He had cramps in his legs, and the afternoon's jovial mood had been replaced with feelings of loneliness, gloom, and longing. Longing for what? Perhaps death. Perhaps relief. An ideal life. What expectation? What he had always been waiting for. Just as much as death. Twin spirit with death, his double. Whatever it was, it was because of that book and the answer that it provided: Tomorrow—it will not be there.

His watch was over, but he could not make himself wake the Lieutenant up. He thought: Let this be another night added to all those nights of sleeplessness and anxiety. What would he lose?

The Lieutenant's eyes darted under his half-shut eyelids and his lips moved. He could pick out certain words but could not understand the entire sentence. It was choppy and disconnected. What sort of creature was this weak, scrawny man?

He wanted to stay awake until morning. He wanted to see tomorrow, lest what was said in the book would turn out to be true. He was afraid to shut his eyes. A superstitious fear had made him neurotic. He would have to be freed from the claws of groundless apprehension.

When his eyelids became heavy, he said to himself that he had to wake up the Lieutenant before he fell sleep. He thought that death would not dare come to a sleeping man before the eyes of a person who was awake. He did not know when the radio fell out of his hand. He tried to get up once or twice, but he could not. It was as if he were nailed down to the ground. And the rats came. They were climbing over each other. And the bayonet that cut a scrawny little finger to take off the ring. Sawing the flesh and bone, and the finger continuing to resist the sharp edge of the bayonet without being injured. The hand that was cutting the finger with the bayonet got tired. Perhaps it was frightened of the hoard of attacking gray rats. He stuck the bayonet into the ground. He took the finger and forced it backward: Crack . . .

He suddenly awoke. Sweat was pouring from his skin. The Lieutenant was sitting by his side, shaking him. The radio was crackling under his body. He looked at the dark, cold bunker with sleepy eyes. Where was he? He raised his hand and saw the turquoise ring.

Grumbling, the Lieutenant pulled out the radio from under him and turned it off.

"You should know there isn't a market nearby for me to get something to eat."

He was still trembling from the dream that he'd had.

"I don't know when I fell asleep."

He got out from under the blanket. The Lieutenant began exercising. Reluctantly and sleepily, he boiled some water and brought it along with a box of cookies and put them on the table.

The Lieutenant crouched up by the Coleman water cooler and splashed a handful of water on his face.

"So you stood watch even when it was my turn."

"I fell asleep. And I don't know when."

"What difference does it make? Who's going to show up here?"

After breakfast, he smoked a cigarette and then got up to go out. He pushed the blanket aside and wanted to open the door. The door was stuck tightly and would not move. It was as if they had sealed it with a mortar of gypsum and cement. The Lieutenant was busy with his work, unconcerned. He was brushing his teeth with pineapple juice. The radio was playing a military march.

He thought that the door must be frozen or a rock or something had rolled and fallen against it. But he realized that that was not the case. Snow had piled up in the ditch behind the door and he could not get out.

The Lieutenant came to help him, panting. Both of them tried to push the door, which opened a foot or so, and puffs of snow blew in. Through the crack of the door, the whiteness of the cold snow met the eye. The only palpable thing was the freezing cold.

He said: "We're stuck. We're stuck in here."

The Lieutenant laughed: "Your corpse, like frozen meat, will not rot. Aren't you happy?"

And he went and fetched the small shovel, and through the crack of the door began to remove the snow. He was panting and sweat was streaming down behind his ears. They took turns shoveling several times until finally a path was cleared. Outside, the snow and ice were wreaking havoc.

Once the opening in front of the bunker was cleared, they opened a narrow path in the snow to the edge of the precipice. The whiteness of the snow hurt their eyes, and cold cut their skin like shards of glass.

By the time they had cleared the area behind the bunker to use it as a toilet, half the day had passed.

They returned to the bunker and had some tea. The Lieutenant was still panting, but he was refreshed and in good spirits. When he finished his tea, he took the binoculars and went out. A few minutes later, he returned frustrated, and radioed coordinates to the base with the transmitter.

They could not do anything but sit and wait in the bunker.

Near sunset, he felt that his heart was about to stop. The Lieutenant neither talked nor did anything else. He was reading a magazine silently and yawning.

"How about a game of cards?"

The Lieutenant grumbled: "I don't feel like it."

"Then let's box."

The Lieutenant looked at him over the magazine. "Are you nuts?"

"Then what should we do?"

"Go to sleep!"

Then, as if he had remembered something, he said: "Nothing is worse than futility."

He put down the magazine, crawled toward the radio transmitter, and reported their coordinates.

"Now go out and watch the fireworks."

He went back angrily to where he was sitting before and picked up the magazine.

The sound of two consecutive explosions shook the bunker.

The Lieutenant, with a "whooo," picked up the transmitter again.

"Good job . . . Three more with the same coordinates."

He thought the Lieutenant was confused. He got up and filled the lantern with kerosene and left the bunker. The ground under his feet shook three times. He ran on the narrow path and stopped at the edge of the precipice. It seemed that the echo of the artillery rounds had frozen in the middle of the hills. And he felt his vision getting blurred and his ears buzzing. Terrified, he retreated from the edge of the precipice.

The sky seemed blue and the wind was howling between the rocks. He went behind the bunker and relieved himself. Tiny flakes of snow were falling sporadically. But the sky was clear and no clouds could be seen. He was no longer certain of anything. He felt that the ground had given way under his feet. No matter what, he must busy himself with something.

What was he remembering? Perhaps he remembered a drawing in one of his childhood textbooks. He took his gloves out of his pocket and put them on. He jumped into the ditch in front of the bunker, picked up the shovel, and came out. He stopped for a moment, and then began working relentlessly.

Now the snow had piled up. The Lieutenant was still inside the bunker and had not made a sound. It seemed that he had sent the coordinates just to spite him. When he was taking the shovel, he had seen from the corner of the blanket covering the opening to the bunker that the Lieutenant had pulled up a blanket over his head and had the radio next to his ear.

He pounded the pile of snow with the back of the shovel and evened it out. His snowman was gradually coming to life. Big, with an awesome presence. It was erected as the darkness of night was falling. It had thick arms, a hefty body, and a cold heart.

He said out loud: "Now that I have created him from the snow of the sky, I must blow the spirit of life into him."

He was standing on the roof of the bunker, looking at the large head of the snowman. A yellow light spread from the opening of the bunker onto the snowman. He came down, looked around, but did not see any pieces of rock or clay. They had all been buried under the snow. He went into the bunker, made a hole in one of the sandbags, and came out with a fistful of sand.

The Lieutenant shouted: "What are you doing?"

"'Let the Earth be filled with creatures.' Come and look!"

He got on the top of the bunker again and put in the snowman's eyes. When he came down, he found the stony glare of his creation cold, horrified, and stunned.

The Lieutenant came out with the lantern in his hand and was taken aback seeing the snowman. A strange smile froze on his lips. He raised the lantern and said in a deep voice: "We have created enmity between you and man. He might possibly strike your head with a spade and you shall destroy him with the cold."

He took the lantern from the Lieutenant and looked at him bitterly. The Lieutenant was laughing madly and punching the snowman.

"Don't think that you are the only one who knows all these big words. I know all the Holy Books by heart."

He ran laughing behind the bunker, and from there he said deliberately: "Take the lantern inside. It's dangerous."

He did not want to hear the Lieutenant's voice. He went into the bunker. He opened a can of food and started eating alone. When the Lieutenant came in, he was taken aback. He said: "I'm not hungry."

Then he went and leaned against the wall of the bunker, lit a cigarette, and looked at him like a hungry dog.

He finished his food and saw that the Lieutenant was pretending to sleep with the cigarette between his lips. He pulled out the lit cigarette from between the Lieutenant's lips, took a few deep puffs, and crushed it in the food can. He then turned down the flame of the lantern and unconsciously brushed his teeth with pineapple juice, like the Lieutenant, and went back and lay down on the blanket.

The bunker was cold and spiritless.

He shut his eyes. The words that the Lieutenant had read in the fortune-telling book resonated in his ears, and he saw the advancing black line scattered on the gray plain, spreading out everywhere.

He thought: Why did I tell the Lieutenant about the ring?

Since then, the sunburned face of that young boy had

been constantly before his eyes. Then his eyelids became heavy and again the rats . . .

The Lieutenant stuck his head into the bunker and shouted: "You're still asleep! Get up, man. The fellow is almost here."

He yawned and looked at the Lieutenant indifferently. He still thought that the Lieutenant was pulling his leg and wanted to wake him up.

"Get up. It's one of those tough Republican Guard guys who's coming up here. Get up. He'll be here in half an hour."

He came out from under the blanket. The Lieutenant's apprehension had also infected him. He splashed some water on his face and, along with the Lieutenant, started to straighten up the bunker. When the Lieutenant began to shave, he picked up the binoculars and left the bunker.

The Lieutenant was telling the truth. Someone was plowing the snow with his chest, like a wolf, and climbing straight up the mountain effortlessly.

When he lowered the binoculars, the Lieutenant was standing next to him with razor cuts on his face.

"With cold water, you can't do a better job than this," he said. Then he added, laughing, "You should be grateful that you can't grow a beard."

He was offended by what the Lieutenant said, but he did not say anything. Their relationship had become more formal since the previous evening.

The Lieutenant said: "I'm sure that they have become suspicious of us. Good thing that I sent those few coordinates."

He then turned around toward the precipice and pointed with his finger.

"Look. They're still there. Maybe they have been stuck in the snow for these couple of days."

In the direction of the Lieutenant's finger, the continuous black line on the completely white plain was spreading out even more.

The Lieutenant shouted: "Do you think that when he sees them he won't say anything? I know these party members. The first thing that he'll do is report to the base. Then we will have to deal with the Army Intelligence Unit and interrogation, or we may be sent to even worse places . . ."

"They are not military forces. We shouldn't waste bullets on them for no good reason."

"Was the kid whose ring you cut off from his finger a soldier?"

The Lieutenant's words penetrated his heart like a dagger.

"You're making excuses."

"Watch what you say in front of this guy. I have been in the war from the beginning. I have studied law. I know what I'm talking about."

"What should we do now?"

"Don't you worry. I am your superior. I am the one who is accountable." Then he pointed to the snowman, "And remove this scarecrow from in front of the bunker. I don't want him to have an excuse."

He had become subservient to the Lieutenant. He brought the shovel and with one movement chopped off the head of the snowman. Then he kicked its body and stomped on it, mixing it in with the snow on the ground.

Chapter Four

❀

"**I** have been assigned to help out with observation here."
These were the first words that came out of the mouth of the Republican Guard Second Lieutenant. He was standing in front of the bunker, panting. When he went to the precipice to look at the plain, his back was soaking wet with sweat. It seemed as if he had climbed all the way through the snow in one breath.

The Lieutenant stood next to the Second Lieutenant and gazed at the white plain. The black line of nomads could be seen more clearly on the all-white background.

When the Second Lieutenant turned to the Lieutenant, the whites of his eyes seemed red. The Lieutenant was whistling, unconcerned and looking ahead.

The Second Lieutenant said: "From the Army Intelligence Unit, the assignment . . ."

He swallowed the rest of what he was saying. Obviously, he had mentioned the Intelligence Unit in order for the Lieutenant to understand who was in charge.

The Lieutenant moved away from the edge of the precipice a few steps and winked at him with his back to the Second Lieutenant. His eyes clearly said: You can see that my guess was right.

The Second Lieutenant was still looking at the plain, and his face was turning redder every moment. With his average height, long face, and delicate neck, the Lieutenant was looking contemptuously at the robust Second Lieutenant.

He was standing between the Lieutenant and the Second Lieutenant, confused. He did not know what to do. He had never expected the Lieutenant to be so self-assured as to treat a Republican Guard Second Lieutenant in this way.

Turning to him, the Lieutenant told him to go to the bunker and prepare something to eat.

He rushed to the bunker without any hesitation. He was happy to be free from the hostile eyes of the Second Lieutenant and the indifferent behavior of the Lieutenant. He picked up a few cans of food and put them in the water in the kettle to warm up. He did not want things to appear too comfortable. He could hear the voice of the Lieutenant from outside reluctantly explaining the status of the region to the Second Lieutenant.

He went and stood by the door of the bunker, listening. The water in the kettle was boiling and making bubbling sounds. It had dawned on him that things were not going right and that something tragic might occur. The Second Lieutenant's face was not friendly at all.

"You are not performing your duty. The enemy is marching before your eyes, and then . . ."

"The snow destroyed all of our plans. Since yesterday we have been waiting to clear a path through it in front of the bunker, in order not to suffocate inside."

For a moment the conversation stopped. The sound of the boiling water inside the bunker was like that of poisonous vapors bubbling in a swamp. Then he heard the voice of the Second Lieutenant, who was asking for binoculars.

"Apparently, you have come to war reluctantly. The enemy is moving freely in front of you . . ."

"But I told you . . ."

"All of these are excuses. I . . ."

He heard the nervous laughter of the Lieutenant.

"The principles of artillery say something else. Why do you think they gave me the rank of an officer? Do you expect us to shoot at every Iranian that we see? I know my duty."

"I will report everything to the base."

"Then what are you waiting for?"

When he heard the sound of their footsteps getting closer, he took the food cans out of the water, burning his hand and splattering hot water on his clothes. The Second Lieutenant entered the bunker angrily, following the Lieutenant, and cast a disapproving glance around.

With a very sarcastic look, the Lieutenant took out a cigarette and sat on the ammunition box.

He opened the cans of food and poured them into the frying pan, and then placed them on the box next to the Second Lieutenant.

The Second Lieutenant looked at him angrily.

"I have not come here to party. Turn on the radio transmitter."

He looked at the Lieutenant with hesitation. The Lieutenant did not say anything or make any gesture as to what he should do. He puffed at the cigarette and blew the smoke calmly in front of him.

"Someone who has come here to help with the observation should certainly know his job."

Frustrated, the Second Lieutenant went to the Lieutenant. His face and his hands revealed his outrage. The Lieutenant laughed in his face, then turned around toward him and gestured to him to leave the bunker.

At the Lieutenant's gesture, he left the bunker most willingly. With two superior officers behaving with hostility toward each other, he would be between a rock and a hard place. He sighed with relief and saw that his knees were shaking. His nerves were badly shot. Out of fear or excitement, he did not know. The Lieutenant's reaction had shocked him. He thought: You can only figure people out under particular circumstances.

Now he regretted his demeaning attitude toward the Lieutenant the day before. He crouched up next to the bunker and looked at the deep furrow that the Second Lieutenant had left behind in the snow. The voices inside the bunker were becoming louder.

"If they do not trust us, why did they give us such a great responsibility?"

"The issue is not trust. Everyone must perform his duty well. This place is full of empty cans of food. All you did was eat and sleep."

"Apparently you have forgotten that you are talking to a superior officer."

"I do not respect anyone who betrays his homeland."

And again there was silence. Then there was the sound of the Lieutenant striking a match. His heart began palpitating.

"Watch your mouth. I am a law student and my rank is superior to yours."

"That is why the enemy is marching in front of you and you are just sitting by doing nothing."

"Those are a bunch of women and children. Our villagers also cross down there."

"Turn on the radio transmitter and report the coordinates."

"I did that when it was time for it. It is not necessary now. If you know how to, go ahead and do it on your own authority."

The Second Lieutenant raised his voice; he was cursing and moving toward the radio transmitter.

"But this does not work."

"It's cold and damp, so it's not working."

"This is an excuse. You could ask them to destroy all of them with mortar fire."

"That place is not within the range of mortar fire. It is at least twenty kilometers away."

"You traitors! All you've done here is eat and sleep."

The situation was becoming critical, and his bones were shaking from the cold. He got up and began pacing back and forth. He knew that the Lieutenant himself had rigged the radio transmitter. He had seen him do it when the Second Lieutenant was climbing up; the Lieutenant had gone to the radio transmitter for a moment and come back.

The Second Lieutenant shouted: "I will report you and you'll get what you deserve!"

For a moment, he heard the Lieutenant laughing. Then he felt the bunker shake, and he heard the sound of something falling and breaking, and then the sound of shouting and cursing.

He went toward the bunker. He hesitated for a few moments. Now he was sure that the Second Lieutenant had attacked the Lieutenant and they were wrestling.

He went inside. The Second Lieutenant, with his huge body, had fallen on the Lieutenant and was trying to choke him with both hands.

The Lieutenant's eyes were bulging out of their sockets and his lips had turned blue. With fear and horror in his eyes, he was trying to remove the Second Lieutenant's hands from his neck, but the Second Lieutenant had the better of him and was choking him with utter hatred.

He pulled the Second Lieutenant from behind to separate them. The Lieutenant was shouting and asking for help. The Second Lieutenant turned around and punched him in the face. He staggered and fell on the empty box of ammunition, and then rolled onto the frying pan full of food. His hand got greasy, and when he tried to get up, he fell again. A severe pain ran through his spine. At the same time, he heard the Lieutenant's voice, which seemed to be coming from the bottom of a well, pleading for help.

He managed to get up with difficulty, and once again attacked the Second Lieutenant, grabbing his overcoat from the back and pulling it.

The Lieutenant was struggling in the grip of the large, dark hands of the Second Lieutenant. His tongue was sticking out and his mouth was foaming. For a moment, his eyes locked onto the pleading eyes of the Lieutenant.

He punched the Second Lieutenant's neck, cursed him and pulled him.

In one movement, the Second Lieutenant tossed him over his head next to the Lieutenant and kicked his face with the heel of his boot. The sound of bones cracking resonated in his head and blood gushed out of his nose.

He could not see anything. He tried to grab hold of something to get up. The sound of the Lieutenant's moaning was gradually fading. His hand touched the rifle.

Involuntarily, he picked up the rifle, turned around shouting, and started shooting at the Second Lieutenant, who had immediately held out his arms in fear.

His ears were filled with the sound of the explosion of the shots; the smell and smoke of gunpowder made him cough. He threw the rifle to the ground in disgust, stood up in horror, and grabbed the sandbags.

The Second Lieutenant had fallen on his back to the ground in the bunker. His face was mutilated and bloody as he lay there quietly, without any movement, like a log.

Chapter Five

❈

He did not have the courage to return to the bunker. He was standing outside, shivering from the cold. He could not believe that he had killed the Second Lieutenant. Everything had happened so suddenly. The Lieutenant was chain-smoking and pacing in the narrow path in the snow. His face had been disfigured and his hair was disheveled. The bluish imprints of the Second Lieutenant's fingers were visible on his thin red neck.

How excruciatingly the time was passing! He had lost track of the hour. His mouth had a bitter taste and he no longer felt like smoking. He was shifting on his feet and trying to avoid eye contact with the Lieutenant.

Night was approaching, and if they were to stand outside as they were, the blood would freeze in their veins. The Lieutenant was not paying any attention to him at all. The snow was pounded down under his feet and sparkled like polished metal. Every few minutes he coughed. Holding his neck, he bent over and spit out blood on the snow.

He looked through the opening of the bunker. The lantern was turned off; but in the semidarkness inside, the large, motionless legs of the Second Lieutenant, clad in olive-colored trousers, were visible. He thought they had to do something. When the Lieutenant reached him, he stopped him.

"It was out of my control. I don't know what happened."

The Lieutenant was confused and in a state of disbelief, as if he was unaware of anything that had happened.

"I swear to God it was out of my control. Now what should we do?"

The veins in the Lieutenant's neck swelled up: "You killed

him. You! They will execute you, you wretch!"

"You told me to. You wanted help. He was choking you."

The Lieutenant shook his head madly. "No. I said no such thing. You are lying."

"You got caught in a mess, and now you're trying to deny it. You are also involved."

"Me?"

"Yes, you. If I had not shot him, you would not be alive now."

The Lieutenant threw his cigarette butt quickly onto the snow.

"Suppose I told you to. Don't you have any brains? You are the murderer, not me."

"You should have said this when you were struggling, not now."

The Lieutenant shrugged his shoulders. His entire body was visibly shaking. He looked as if he had lost as much weight in this half a day as he might in several months. His face, with cuts from the razor, and his bruised neck looked pitiable.

"Well, now we have to find a solution."

He felt that the Lieutenant was giving up. He lowered his voice.

"A solution? If there is a speck of honor in you, you won't let me get into trouble."

"Why don't you understand? It was you who shot him, not me. In fact, who told you to meddle in our business?"

"I did this for you. He was choking you."

"Don't try to make me feel indebted to you. I wish you hadn't done anything for me. I wish you had let him finish me off . . . Now that the situation has turned out worse, we will have to die like dogs."

He thought he should compromise with the Lieutenant somehow. It was a risky situation; and hunger and cold were making it worse.

"What do you think we should do with the body now?"

"The body?"

"Why are you doing this? Have you gone mad? Yes, the body. The same guy who was choking you and now is lying on his back inside."

The Lieutenant looked into the bunker and quickly turned his face away.

"The lantern has gone out."

"What is it? Are you afraid?"

"Yes, I'm afraid of the corpse."

"But you have killed so many people. You're used to having corpses around you."

"This one is different. This is called a crime, murder."

The Lieutenant's rationale made him laugh.

"Murder or crime, whatever; this is what we do. Now we should go inside and light the lantern."

He entered the bunker first, followed by the Lieutenant, who was coughing. They struck a match quickly, and then turned up the flame of the lantern. The yellow light spread over the crushed face of the Second Lieutenant; it was covered in coagulated blood.

The Lieutenant vomited.

"We have run out of fuel. We have to survive the night somehow without freezing to death."

The Lieutenant raised his head: "The night?"

"Yes. We have nothing to use to heat up the place, except for this empty box of ammunition and the ceiling beams."

The Lieutenant said: "You think there will be a tomorrow?"

The words from the fortune-telling book popped into his head: Tomorrow—it will not be there. He told the Lieutenant: "Don't jinx it! Help me drag the body outside."

He pulled out the frying pan from under the corpse and rolled the body onto the greasy blanket, which was covered with bits of food. The Lieutenant stood watching.

"Don't just stand there."

They took the two ends of the blanket and lifted the corpse. The Lieutenant tripped and the greasy corner of the blanket slipped out of his hand.

"It's so heavy, the damned thing!"

"Dead bodies are heavy. Don't you know this, even though you *ordered* so many to be killed?"

Again they took the two ends of the blanket, and dragged the corpse to the opening of the bunker. The Lieutenant went outside and pulled on the blanket. The head of the corpse fell out, and its muddy boots stuck out from the other end.

The Lieutenant shouted: "Push! It's stuck."

He put his head under the cold, heavy corpse and forced it out in one push. The corpse fell with its face on the snow. The Lieutenant stepped back. Coagulated blood spread over the snow.

The Lieutenant shouted: "You are worse than a butcher!"

"Sink or swim. We've got to get rid of it. What are you waiting for? Come and help!"

They could see their breath in the frigid air as they dragged the corpse on the snow toward the precipice. A line of blood was being drawn on the snow, and the black claws of the Second Lieutenant seemed to be scratching the snow and grabbing it to prevent them from taking him further.

"Push him down."

The Lieutenant was holding the corpse at the edge of the precipice, shaking.

"I said, let him go. Why are you holding on to him?"

In a trembling voice, the Lieutenant said: "We are done for."

He took the Lieutenant's hand and pulled him away. The corpse rolled on its side on the snow and went down, along with pieces of rock and puffs of snow. The bottom of the precipice was dark and shadowy, but the sound of the rolling rocks and the tumbling corpse could be heard clearly.

He raised his head, and for a moment he saw a fire burning in the distance, with the embers rising into the sky. Something in his stomach churned and fell. He heard the Lieutenant and saw him lying down by the edge of the precipice vomiting bile. He grabbed him under his arms and lifted him.

He dropped the blanket over the opening of the bunker and helped the Lieutenant lie down on the ground. His hands were numb from the cold. He rolled a blanket and placed it under the Lieutenant's head.

The Lieutenant opened his eyes and looked at him pleadingly.

"Would you like me to get you some water?"

"No."

When he turned around to sit down, he stepped into the solidified grease at the bottom of the frying pan, slipped and fell. He picked up the frying pan angrily, went out of the bunker, and threw it among the rocks with a shout. The flickering of the fire on the horizon was brighter this time, and mysterious shadows seemed to be circling it. He ran into the bunker in terror. He picked up the fortune-telling book and tore it to pieces.

The Lieutenant looked at him through sagging eyelids.

"What are you doing?"

"It's all the fault of this damn book of bad omens." He ran and hit the Lieutenant in the face with the torn pieces of the book. "Tell me the truth. Did you also see it?"

"See what?"

"The fire." And he pointed outside.

"Have you gone mad?"

He shouted: "It was all your fault! Why did you treat him like that? You were boasting about your rank. You wanted to show off to me . . . Your foolish arrogance caused us to get into trouble like this."

"I did my duty. You should not have interfered in

our business. It's my fault that I treated you well from the beginning."

He grabbed the Lieutenant by the collar.

"I will not let you blame everything on me."

In a sickly voice, the Lieutenant said: "I don't want to blame everything on you. But you killed him, not me."

He squeezed the Lieutenant's collar in his fist and shook him.

"It was for your sake. You told me to save you. You were dying . . . You rigged the radio transmitter. You think I don't know? You wanted to show the guy that you're somebody. Senior-year law student! Now you will have to die of fear."

The Lieutenant's head was wobbling on his thin neck and he was trembling. He let go of his collar. The Lieutenant fell on his back and groaned.

"I will take whatever comes. I promise you, on my honor. Now, leave me alone; let me think a little."

He left the Lieutenant alone and went out of the bunker. Darkness hung over the mountain and the cold wind was howling among the rocks. He crouched up and lit a cigarette. He was concentrating on what was going on inside the bunker. He cocked his ears, monitoring the slightest sound and action of the Lieutenant.

He got up. The other side of the precipice was engulfed in absolute darkness. He thought that he might have become delusional and that there had been no fire at all that he could have seen. Why had the Lieutenant not seen it? But no, he was certain. He had seen it with his own eyes. And not just once. He felt that his fate was getting closer moment by moment. But he did not know what it would be. The future was still dark and vague to him. And no matter how much he thought, he could not find a way out. He had fallen into the whirlpool headfirst. And the whirlpool was sucking him in and taking him where it wanted. He had killed a Second Lieutenant who was his compatriot and had thrown his body over the precipice. And the witness was lying down in the bunker alive and well, and it was not clear what was going on in his small head and what he was plotting. He would have to concentrate totally. He could not let the Lieutenant get the upper hand. He would certainly try to blame the murder on him. He intended to sacrifice him. If the situation were to end up in court, everyone would undoubtedly take the Lieutenant's side.

He sensed a quiet grating sound coming from inside the bunker. Slowly he slid into the ditch in front of the opening of the bunker and looked through a gap in the blanket. The Lieutenant had crawled on his chest toward the radio transmitter and was messing around with it.

Fear and anger made him tremble from head to toe. He jumped into the bunker, and before the Lieutenant could move, he grabbed the back of his neck and pounded his head against the ammunition box. Blood gushed from the Lieutenant's forehead as he fell down submissively, with his face to the ground. He hid his face in his bloody hands and his shoulders shook.

Into the Lieutenant's ear, he shouted: "I will not let you trick me. I no longer have anything to lose."

The Lieutenant raised his bloody, tearful face.

"It is for her sake. She's only eighteen . . . Do you understand . . . ?"

He shouted: "Eighteen! Stupid jerk. Maybe now she's sitting and thinking about me."

He punched the Lieutenant on the back of his neck.

"You thought I just came out from under a bush? That no one is waiting for me? That I do not want to live? Why are you pretending to be an innocent victim? I killed that animal for your sake. For your sake."

Blood rushed to his face. He bent over and grabbed the Lieutenant's collar from behind and lifted him.

"Tell me the truth. What were you doing with the radio transmitter?"

The Lieutenant was struggling and not answering.

"If you don't tell me, I'll kill you. There will be one less dog for me to worry about."

The Lieutenant released himself from his grasp with difficulty and crawled into the corner of the bunker like a little child.

"I wanted to fix the radio transmitter. That's all."

"You are lying, you dog."

He knocked the Lieutenant down and pressed his foot on his head. Blood splattered from the Lieutenant's forehead onto the sandbags.

"I wanted to snitch on you. I wanted to save myself. Is this what you wanted to hear?"

He removed his foot from the Lieutenant's head and collapsed on the ground.

The Lieutenant sobbed continuously, his face covered with blood. The wind was blowing in through the opening of the bunker, churning puffs of snow inside.

"I admit it. You killed him for my sake. But we only have two choices. Either we both take the blame for the murder or one of us will be sacrificed. If the weather were not as bad as it is, somehow we would get ourselves to the enemy forces. But it is not possible to do so. In front of us, there is the precipice, and behind us are our own forces . . ."

He thought that the Lieutenant was trying to sweet-talk him and was looking for another opportunity to pull the wool over his eyes. There was no guarantee that he would not change his mind once they got down there. If he told the straight truth, he was the one who had shot the Second Lieutenant. It would not be the first time a soldier had been a scapegoat. He was a law student; he could save his own skin. And he certainly had many relatives and friends. He said:

"Either you or me. Only one of us should take the blame for the murder."

The Lieutenant looked at him. He had a cigarette between his lips, and he was wiping the blood from his face with a handkerchief. Then he got up. He tossed the bloody handkerchief into a corner, crushed the cigarette on the blanket under his foot, picked up his overcoat and threw it over his shoulder.

"I got the radio transmitter going. I will let you have the first go at it. I will go outside. You have five minutes to contact the base and report the story as you wish. After five minutes, if you are not able to do it, I will do it the way I want to."

As he was leaving the bunker, he said: "Agreed?"

"Agreed."

The Lieutenant disappeared into the darkness outside the bunker. A cold wind was blowing snowflakes through the doorway.

He brought the lantern and sat next to the radio transmitter. It seemed a fair solution.

He picked up the receiver. By no means did he intend to sacrifice himself for the Lieutenant. He had committed murder for the sake of the Lieutenant, not for his own welfare. He did not want to think about anything else at all. He was afraid of himself.

He was trying to establish contact. It crossed his mind that the problem might not be that simple. He put the receiver back. The Lieutenant was much cleverer than he had thought, even if it was for the sake of his eighteen-year-old. Surely, he already had a plan. He knew his way around, and he certainly understood the vague language of the law better than he did.

He stood up. He had to think. The slightest mistake could cost him his life. And the harsh death that he had frequently envisioned. He wanted to die the way he wanted to. The law was not for the weak.

He looked out the opening of the bunker. The red glow of the Lieutenant's cigarette was quite visible in the middle of the ice storm. Just like a target, something to shoot at. He was standing sideways toward the precipice, and the wind was blowing the flaps of his overcoat.

He raised his hand to his face. What should he do? He went back to the radio transmitter. His eyes fell on the Lieutenant's bloody handkerchief. He picked up the radio and turned the knob. The voice of the announcer filled the bunker. He turned off the radio and placed it between the sandbags. It was no longer of use to anyone, neither to him nor to the Lieutenant. He looked around and saw the shiny rifle with its worn out stock under the light of the lantern. What difference would it make? Would the Lieutenant be the first one?

He picked up the rifle and stood in front of the bunker with his legs apart, and clicked the breechblock loud enough for the Lieutenant to hear it and get ready to do whatever he decided to do.

The Lieutenant was standing motionless, with the cigarette between his lips.

He released the safety lock. He knelt on the ground and aimed the barrel at the red tip of the cigarette.

When he stood up, the Lieutenant had been swallowed in the darkness of the precipice.

Chapter Six

❀

When he opened his eyes, he thought that he would see the Lieutenant brushing his teeth with fruit juice, just like always.

He removed the blankets from on top of him. His entire body was numb. The lantern was out, and the gray light of dawn, along with snow, poured into the bunker. He stretched. The fateful moment had already arrived, and his intuition had not failed him. He got up. With peace of mind, he went to the radio transmitter and tested it. It was in working order. He folded the blankets carefully and arranged them in a corner. He wanted to eat something, but he had no appetite. He had an unpleasant bitter taste in his mouth. He picked up a fistful of snow and stuffed it into his mouth. His bones shivered. He walked over the snow accumulation inside the bunker and went out. The snowstorm had covered the small path that they had made. He walked through the snow, went behind the bunker, and returned, empty and light. He took off his clothes piece by piece, carefully, and stark naked went into the middle of the fresh snow. His body was warm. He knelt on the snow and washed himself. The skin on his body seemed red from being rubbed with handfuls of snow. He was not shivering at all. Neither from fear nor from cold.

He stood up. He came back and put his clothes on. Now he felt cold. He remembered the death scene that he had witnessed: The young man with curly hair was tied to a tree. Someone whose face could not be seen read the verdict. The young man began to tremble and to plead. Between his legs got wet. He called out to his mother, and asked for water. They brought him water in a red plastic pitcher and poured it into his throat. The young man straightened himself up and gazed at the barrels of the rifles. He was no longer moving. Perhaps he was already dead, before they killed him. They came and blindfolded him with a black cloth. When the sound of the shots was heard, for a moment the young man's nose turned upwards. As if he was sniffing the air to fill his lungs.

Now he was reading the verdict himself and issuing the order to fire. Standing at the edge of the precipice. He had calculated the specifications of the area precisely. A maximum of six rounds would strike the top of the precipice. And he was standing there, on top of the huge rocks.

He went inside the bunker. He picked up the radio transmitter and reported the coordinates: six rounds, with specifications.

He got up. He opened a can of pineapple juice and drank the liquid to the last drop. He crushed the can in his hand and threw it outside the bunker. The can rolled down the snow bank.

He came out of the bunker. He could still hear the can rolling. He took off his overcoat, folded it, and put it on the low roof of the bunker. He was too hot.

He took a deep breath and his chest filled with air.

The whistle of the first round resonated in the cold, clean air of the mountain. He still had a lot of time. Calmly, he walked to the edge of the precipice and saw the snow shooting up into the sky, along with smoke and fire.

He went to the top of a rock. Now the precipice was under his foot. Without anyone to humiliate him. And the Second Lieutenant and the Lieutenant were lying down at the bottom, comfortable and pain free. And the plain before him, empty and white.

The second round howled as it passed over his head.

It hit a little past "my tree." The tree shook and its dry leaves scattered in the air, twirling down calmly. He felt his legs trembling. He took control of himself. He would have to have endurance. He thought about his mother, and that lock of hair on the forehead. And "my tree," the leaves of which were still flying in the air and falling on the stained, ruffled surface of the snow.

The third round hit the rock below him.

The ground shook under his feet. He could hardly keep his balance. Large rocks with flying snow rolled down speedily.

He looked at the village houses behind the trees. From the roofs of some a thin line of blue smoke was rising into the air. He sniffed the air. It smelled like fresh bread, warm and delicious.

The fourth round took off half of a rock protrusion, and the rock crumbled with a horrifying sound. Small pieces of stone, frozen snow, and ice splattered on his face.

Not much time left.

The plain was filled with men dressed in black. With sticks in their hands, they were moving forward slowly. He took off the turquoise ring and threw it toward them. They continued advancing. Sorrowful and nervous, with torches in their hands.

He felt the heat of the fifth round on his face.

He said: "And the coup de grâce!"

He shut his eyes. The men dressed in black were behind his closed eyelids. They were advancing closer and closer. They formed a circle around "my tree" and began to chant. He could not hear them well. He perked up his ears.

He heard the sound of the sixth round.

Spring 1995

An Interview with the Author

❀

In 2006, when I was translating *Fortune Told in Blood*, I contacted Davud Ghaffarzadegan and asked him to send me some background information on himself and his views as a writer. In response, he sent me the following interview conducted by Yusef Alikhani for a journal. Interestingly, the interview not only reveals the author's views on literature and life, but also provides insight into the general atmosphere in which creative artists live and work in Iran.

ALIKHANI: My generation, which is approaching thirty years of age, is familiar with the name Davud Ghaffarzadegan through his stories for adolescents. I will never forget following [the magazine serial] *Shadows and Long Night* every month. Even though this story was published as a book under the same title, the question is why you categorize it as a story for adults and not adolescents?

GHAFFARZADEGAN: To tell you the truth, I don't understand such categorizations. It seems to me that every story first has to prove that it is a story, in other words, that it is a story and nothing else. The subsequent question of who would read the story has nothing to do with the writer. Recently, someone wrote, "Ghaffarzadegan writes for adolescents, so why is he acting like he also writes for adults?" More interestingly, the same person several years ago wrote an article about *We Are Three Persons* in which, with the same presuppositions, he also regarded all the characters as adolescents. It's true that there are as many readings as there are readers, but the problem is that sometimes someone's likes and dislikes result in extratextual proclamations, and something that he or she wants or does not want is inserted into or omitted from the text. Even more interesting things have happened. Critics have rejected one of my so-called adolescent books under the pretext that it is for adults, and they have dismissed it in their assessments. A specific example occurred in regard to *Shadows and Long Night*, which apparently was not considered suitable for readers of any age group.

Our problem is that we do not appreciate individuality and cannot accept anything but conformity and following like sheep. You either have to play the game with preset rules or be marginalized.

ALIKHANI: We will get to this issue, but regarding *Shadows and Long Night* . . .

GHAFFARZADEGAN: To me, that story is not finished yet; four hundred or five hundred pages of it have been written, and the rest remains to be written before we can see what it turns out to be.

Also, because the text was depressing, publishers for adolescents would not publish it, following the recommendation of their reviewers, and because the narrator of the story was an adolescent, publishers for adults were hesitant about it. I've never understood these rules. I wrote a story, and it didn't matter to me what publisher would publish it or for what audience. But eventually the book was published, and even went through a second printing. In the final analysis, a story is like words tossed on the ground that are eventually picked up by those who want them. I think that there is something wrong with a story that is written for a particular audience, and we should question its authenticity. After all, the writer of such a story is either trying to be didactic or ideological, or trying to speak out of both sides of his mouth at the same time. Or, so to speak, he is trying to pose as an intellectual. And all of this is done in order to face the *Thousand-and-One-Nights* world in which he fears for his life and hopes to see the sunrise on the following day.

ALIKHANI: And, of course, after a few years, when we'd left behind our teenage years, *We Are Three Persons* was published, a book that belongs to the category of stories for adults.

GHAFFARZADEGAN: Of course, if the criteria are adolescence, youth, and other ages of your growing up, we will have to wait. In other words, I will have to wait. But I want to say that I don't consider myself any particular type of writer; I only try to write stories. I try, but what I want to explain is that sometimes a writer gathers from people's statements that writing for adolescents is easy or, supposedly, non-intellectual, and so on. In a gathering, a friend who writes for adolescents was told sympathetically that, God willing, he would grow up and write thick books for adults. It may be difficult to admit, but the truth is that in no other time in his life does a person feel like he understands as much as he does during his adolescence. And he can't help that. It's the raging hormones and all that. It's like despair during middle age— when a person ignores the fact that he shouldn't eat certain things that create gas but he does, and philosophical despair increases continuously. In fact, writing stories that appeal to adolescents is difficult, even impossible. Forget about the official statistics and popular books that suddenly appear everywhere. Their appearance and disappearance are dubious, similar to the disease SARS; and more than having literary value, they are valuable for psychological research. Look at the books that adolescents read in private. This period of life is a strange age.

On the one hand, you lose the insight of childhood and, on the other, you are pained by the foolish and tedious concerns of adults. Total purgatory.

ALIKHANI: Because of the type of writing you do, you are a writer who has been very much in touch with the true experiences of children and adolescents before they are made into literature. To what extent has this helped your writing?

GHAFFARZADEGAN: In my opinion, the basic theme and subject matter of every writer in some way go back to his own childhood and adolescence. I'm not concerned about writers who, like small children, mimic adults and want to make themselves appear important. I believe that creativity requires thinking like children, and mimicking creativity means making oneself appear important, like politicians. Children have insight in regard to individuals and objects, and this is the height of creativity. In other words, to see everything the way we want it rather than the way others want it, and this is not possible except by not submitting to the rules of the game and, like children, being immersed in the game of what you want. Of course, this is not very much under our control and mostly goes back to our own nature. There are many adults who mimic children.

ALIKHANI: You say that you write stories, and it does not matter whether they are for adults or for adolescents. But when I was reading the stories in your last collection, *The Delriz Girls*, here and there I felt, Davud Ghaffarzadegan is revealing that he is writing for adolescents. Do you agree that this is true?

GHAFFARZADEGAN: I had not concealed myself nor wanted to reveal myself. Some of the stories in this collection were written seven or eight years ago and published in magazines, and also some of them that I wrote in the past few years have been published in magazines. As I said, this is not the issue. This was also the fate of the collections *We Are Three Persons* and *The Secret of the Murder of Mr. Mir*, as well as *Fortune Told in Blood*, and it will continue unless I submit to the perversion that they want, uniformity.

ALIKHANI: Perhaps this situation is created because in some of the stories of this collection you employ first-person narrators, not to mention the type of characters and environments that you create.

GHAFFARZADEGAN: You probably mean that because the narrators or the characters of some of the stories are adolescents, such a perception is created, and then from that you want to reach the same conclusion that was reached by the gentleman on the Art Center website, and eventually the same article appeared on Ahmad Gholami's literary page in *Sharq* newspaper. Look, we have stories for adolescents and stories about adolescents. This is the most commonplace, the most obvious, and the most basic categorization that you would expect specialists to understand. Besides, are we supposed to have the same outlook? In fact, I don't have the proper picture of, for example, a thirty-year-old, and I cannot figure out to which nest this bird belongs. My adult characters all seem to have stopped in childhood. For this reason, they are clumsy, innocent, and sometimes foolishly simpleminded or sneaky, and are easily victimized, or masochistic, and their ignorance reveals everything, and with the flick of a finger they are tossed into a whirlpool created for them. None of this has anything to do with stories for children and adolescents.

ALIKHANI: The beginning of each and every one of the stories of this collection is a masterpiece; however, I do not know why, but your refusal to step out of the rules of traditional storytelling is not pleasing.

GHAFFARZADEGAN: I wish there was someone who would tell me what these rules of traditional storytelling are, to soothe my wounds. I think that our outlooks regarding stories—whether traditional or otherwise—are somewhat different; and of course this difference gives variety to our writings, and motivates us to read each other's writings. But I have a suggestion. Let us read all the translated works of Edgar Allan Poe, then also take a look at fiction writing after Poe and see who has done something new that, for example, he did not do. Of course, since Edgar Allan Poe, numerous events have occurred in the world and . . . what I mean is something else. Much of the confusion and the games that recently have started in Iran are old and tired; in fact, they belong to the eighteenth and nineteenth centuries, and like the short-sighted showing off of the nouveau riche, they turn your stomach.

When there is no thought behind the work, the text becomes a ridiculous Punch and Judy show, and becomes one of these multi-voice stories in which one of the characters speaks in a low pitch and another in a high pitch, and incidentally both are out of tune. For now, these games are some sort of response to the chaotic market. Such stories quickly leave the scene and end up on the colorful pages of popular magazines that promote competitions. Writing is not a gimmick. It is different from a magic show and pulling a rabbit out of a hat. And it is not telling entertaining stories for a bunch of people with full stomachs, or for filling the leisure hours of housemaids. It is an internal experience that cannot be duplicated, and everyone reaches it in a different way. No one is refuting anyone else; everyone goes his own way.

ALIKHANI: Considering the environments that you create and your beautiful and unique descriptions, the dialogues do not seem very appropriate to the characters.

GHAFFARZADEGAN: Yes, that is true, because the characters are not suitable to the dialogues that you have in mind. If your reference is outside the story, that is not acceptable. Nowhere in the world do children speak like the children of a single story, for example, "The Delriz Girls." They have metamorphosed out of fear, and like primitive people, deal with words like chants. Or in "All That There Is," by repeating one legend, they want to summon what is lost, the name of which they do not know. Interestingly, one critic of this story is looking for the lost teacher, or in "The Botanist Father," because of the title of the story, he thinks that I haven't written anything about the father and he thinks that Delbar, which is the name of an animal in the story, is a character, or he thought that in the story "Witnesses," because the words "Ali Qapu" are used, the story takes place in Isfahan, and so forth.

ALIKHANI: The eerie climate in the stories of the collection *The Delriz Girls* is very nice. Sometimes the characters are eerie and sometimes the entire climate of the story is eerie, such as the three or four stories at the beginning of the book.

GHAFFARZADEGAN: Yes, in "The Botanist Father," the character of the soldier is apparently eerie; in "The Delriz Girls" and "All That There Is," the entire climate is eerie; and in "The Magic Tree," "Your Name Is Like Spilled Perfume," and "The Lost," I myself am eerie. I like physics because of metaphysics.

ALIKHANI: The use of villages as the locales of the stories is one of your preoccupations, which brings to mind the fact that you were a teacher in such places. To what extent have you tried to make use of locales that are pristine?

GHAFFARZADEGAN: Usually I make a collage of the locale and geography. And contrary to what you think, I'm not very much interested in villages as locales. I think about the people's situation in such places that only provide you with the abundant possibility of being bored to death. The same villages may be a microcosm of metropolises such as Tehran, because I think that we are still enslaved by tribal ideas, and everything that we do, pardon me, is totally like what a country bumpkin does. Precisely like this interview, in which, as Akhavan-Sales would put it, we are facing each other like two closed windows, each of us humming our own tune.

ALIKHANI: The longest story in the collection is "The Magic Tree." Even though it has an interesting subject matter, the tone of the reportage and the speed of the narration are not pleasing to the heart.

GHAFFARZADEGAN: First of all, I do not know what sort of thing the heart is, that something can please or not please it. It is like, "He laughed strangely" or "He heard a strange laugh," which one finds in stories. But, on the whole, it could be as you say. Nevertheless, I think that a person who is caught in such a predicament does not even have the time to swallow his spit. And the high or slow speed of the narration apparently is not something independent of the story, something one can slow down or speed up. But all this aside, is "The Magic Tree" not the story of our fate of the past 150 years?

ALIKHANI: I do not often see Ghaffarzadegan moving in line with the waves of fiction writing today in Iran. It seems that you swim upstream, in the direction that is the reverse of others. Is that not so?

GHAFFARZADEGAN: First of all, I have no idea what wave you are talking about, and second of all, I do not know how to swim at all; I only try not to sink. That's all.